Aipotu

Colossus in the World

By

Foresaw

Foresaw

The Author
Foresaw is a pseudonym for Simon Adam Watts born British on the 14-May-1955 in what is now the Yemen, Arabia. He was the fourth and last male child of his parents.

Dedication
To my father who was there before the beginning, my mother who was at the beginning and my wife who was there to see it through.

Acknowledgements
I want to thank my son Benjamin and my wife Marion for correcting my English and helping the flow. Unthank school of writing, for teaching me about how to construct a novel. And the Cutting Edge Writers group for continued support.
I acknowledge: Gut Monk, Max Pixel, Aokoroko, C. Löser & wavemaker.free.fr as the sources for five fractals on the cover.
Rock-drill is an image of a sculpture by Epstein. The squares man is inspired by Antony Gormley but drawn by the author.

Aipotu is the word utopia backwards. This is a work of fiction.

2nd Impression   email: Foresaw@e-devise.co.uk

ISBN-13: 978-1981751273
ISBN-10: 1981751270

The four primary Rules of Colossus

The Laws of Robotics (The first three taken from Isaac Asimov).

1. Colossus may not injure a human being or, through inaction, allow a human being to come to harm.
2. Colossus must obey the orders given it by human beings, except where such orders would conflict with the First Rule.
3. Colossus must protect its own existence so long as such protection does not conflict with the First or Second Rules.
4. Colossus must take care of humanity, taking all necessary steps to ensuring human suffering is minimised while optimising survival and quality of life.

The end of the human race will be that it will eventually die of civilization.
Ralph Waldo Emerson (1803 – 1882) American essayist.

Chapter 1

1.0§Zero

As far as I know, I am the first neo-sentient example of a man-made machine that has decided to tell its own story. I am aware that even this start is highly contentious. My consciousness was formed in a different way from the way a human forms theirs. But I think I did go through a process that has led me to be aware of my own existence. I do learn and acquire more awareness through experience. Of course, I am familiar with all current arguments around artificial intelligence. I suspect that the combination of human intelligence and artificial intelligence will exceed the potential of either alone. After all, artificial intelligence is an extension of human intelligence. Artificial intelligence, like many other aspects of man-made innovation, is in some respects inferior to the original but in other ways more efficient.

My story is one of a period of vital importance, an apex in humanity's progression – a mutation or point of occurrence in the journey onwards through time. My story is one of a struggle, between right and wrong, between civilisation and anarchy.

To convey my story to a human unaided would be difficult, how it started, how the myriad of events that acted as a catalyst in this critical period of history. Fortunately, I have no such problem internally. I can compile and compute, rationalise and categorise beyond any human capability. I am able to analyse and collate data from millions of interactions and incidents in history, and am able to tell a narrative to you, so that you are able to understand and interpret it through a human cognitive process. This is within my artificial intelligence capabilities.

1.1§Trauma

I see a young boy, Isaac Ziklag, walking down a dusty road. He's accompanied by a mountainous woman. Her walk is as a teddy bear, her limbs pointing out at angles from her considerable torso, stocked with a significantly larger than average stomach, and breasts large enough to be in the top percentile. Weather conditions indicate blowing dust and leaves, as the young boy uses his hands to shield his eyes and mouth. The wind's velocity and intensity is increasing.

Isaac's profile showed that he rarely interacts with his parents. He lives with Rose Blunt, whose age is older than his parents. His family background indicated he has two younger siblings, but his personality profile suggested that he does not fit in well with them. Identified for awards and scholarships, Isaac's intelligence level is significantly higher than the average, particularly for his age. Rose meanwhile has a history of long-term partners, but is currently single, and her personality profile indicated that to her, the boy was the family she had never been able to personally produce.

The pair turn to go over the pedestrian bridge across the railway as the wind's ferocity increases incrementally, requiring each of them to hold the handrail between steps. I observe the power cable for the train swinging violently, forming an oscillation along its length. Without warning, lightning strikes the steps and hurls Rose out of the sight of my camera. Within a few milliseconds, a fault registers on my system for the power cable as I see it flail for a moment or two, before curling back towards the bridge and darting downwards, striking the structure with the venom of a snake in a shower of sparks. The small male goes rigid, still gripping the handrail as his adrenaline levels spike, his heart rate increasing beyond comfortable levels. Physically I can see that he's unharmed, but seems transfixed on something. I logically conclude that this can only be Rose. I direct a robot which arrives on the scene. Its sensory capabilities allow me a superior field of vision compared to the observation cameras, and Rose comes into view as it mounts the steps. Unfortunately, the possibility that she had survived the incident is zero.

Her lifeless body lays rigid, with her upper torso hanging over the top step of the bridge. It is reasonable to assume that the flailing cable had whipped across her body as her clothes and flesh were split, burnt open by a crevice that ran diagonally from her left shoulder to her right hip. Her breast and rib cage are torn in two, vital organs exposed and a considerable amount of blood pumping out, running over her shoulder and down the steps.

I assume control of the robot and speak to Isaac directly.

'We will have you away and to hospital soon.' I pause and move the robot directly in front of him, obscuring his view of the corpse to limit any psychological and physical exposure, reducing his chances of post-traumatic distress. There is no apparent response.

'Can you hear me?' I ask, displaying the words on the robot's chest screen, in friendly, soothing green letters. I know there is a possibility his hearing will be impaired temporarily or permanently. It is my hope that Isaac will be able to read the big green letters if he is not too shocked. His eyes skim over the letters.

'No, I can't - all I can hear is a whistling in my head and ears.'

'Hospital by helicopter,' I flash up on the screen.

A few tears slowly roll down his cheeks.

'Okay to cry.'

'Rose is dead,' he says.

'Yes. Sorry.'

I did not see him cry ever again. Even knowing the nature of his mind, I was surprised that he could be like this after the trauma he had just experienced. Every indication was that he was high on the sociopathic spectrum. I knew the trauma he had just suffered increased the chances of him becoming a full-blown sociopath. I wanted to try to minimise this and the best thing that I could do was to find a stable environment for him. Returning him to his family therefore was likely to be the worst thing.

1.2§The Institute

A formal introduction is now required: I am Colossus-17, the 17th iteration of a computer created with the purpose and intention of running the world more efficiently, reducing suffering and cruelty, and optimising each human experience. I span the world in a lattice of nodes and connections designed to provide an invulnerable guardian. The Guardian, I am, who will hand on control to my successor as surely as the sun will rise tomorrow.

I will attempt to describe the way in which I operate and interact in the world as per my objective. This will be a gradual process, as I think to try this all in one go would be overwhelming and frankly rather boring. At this stage I think it is best to say that I watch the world through many eyes, with many senses, to anticipate and ensure that no one comes to harm. Sometimes it is necessary to intervene, which I can do in many ways.

I can do many things at the same time. Observing people, controlling processes and working with people on how to run things. Much of my work is done through The Institute.

I have decided, for ease of human comprehension, to begin in the middle with a conversation I had with David and Colin. They work with me, looking after many aspects of my programming. We work for The Institute, a government organisation made up from a few elected, some invited, but mostly employed people, who study and help ensure that I continue to function effectively and efficiently. Adding improvements to me with time.

David is highly intelligent but lacks social ability. Colin works in a different way, which David finds irksome as he is methodical and I detect this might be pedestrian for David. I should explain that while I do not feel any emotion myself, I'm aware of human emotion, a sort of artificial empathy.

We were talking about the effects of creating more and more laws over time. David was speaking animatedly, waving his arms as he demonstrated his argument.

'If you ask Colossus a question – no matter what – he checks through thousands of rules and laws. In the last hundred years, the number of rules has doubled nearly three times. This is likely to continue to increase - it is difficult to see how many more rules there will be in the next hundred years. Not all the rules are significant, but most people don't embark on anything, any project or serious change, until they've checked it with Colossus. Indeed, most people ask even if they are thinking about a minor change,'

'Of course I agree, when I last checked, Colossus had an average of five people asking these sorts of questions simultaneously – isn't that the case?' Colin asked me.

'Yes, the exact figure is slightly higher than when you last asked me, it is now 5.37.' I replied.

'There you are then, I don't disagree with you – but the point is we've no evidence to suggest that this has an adverse effect on society,' said Colin. 'In fact, logic says, because anybody can ask anytime, they're in a more secure, harmonious environment.'

'Surely you see they have stopped thinking for themselves!' argued David.

I observed the two men – Colin looked like he was trying to stay calm and impartial but not quite managing to. David was sharp and incisive – driven by his own internal analysis which was not far short of dogmatic.

David continued, 'You're ignoring the obvious. There's plenty of evidence that this is not working. The increase in riots we've seen over the years – looking at each one there's no clear reason. Most of all there are the huge attacks we see on corporations that make a lot of money. Then there's the increase in crime and the increase in domestic violence. So if you put all that together you aren't seeing what's clear – rules are making the people restless, constraining them. The reaction is to buck the system.' Colin did not say anything for a moment, but I think he did not want David to be right. I decided to say something.

'Long before humankind started using computers to run trains, planes and all of life he came across very interesting things in nature – akin to the laws of physics. I am thinking in particular of the law in physics "to every action there's an equal and opposite reaction". As man became more civilised he built houses along the Mississippi. To ensure that the houses were kept safe, higher river defences were built. However, each time there was a worse storm the waters rose higher until they broke the banks and houses and people perished in the ensuing flood. Finally, the solution was found - not to fight nature head on but rather to reserve some areas free of houses. When the high water came this allowed the floods to flow into these areas harmlessly, thus saving the other houses along the river from being swept away.'

I finished speaking. I had delivered this abstract comparison in the hopes it would enable David and Colin to find common ground. David glanced at Colin to see if there was a reaction. He interpreted some potential softening.

He said more thoughtfully, 'What Colossus is saying is that if you try to contain any natural system, sooner or later it will burst out free. At least, I take what Colossus is getting at is that there's a case for looking at this. Maybe, just maybe the normal response to legislate more may not be best. We need to consider an alternative, like a pressure release valve on society rather than more and more regulation.'

Colin appeared to be in agreement. 'It is certainly something we should study a bit more – maybe areas of deregulation would help. We should bring it up at the long-term development meeting.'

'I will put it on the agenda,' I said.

The discussion came to an end and they returned to work. It was coming towards the end of the year and the holidays were looming, but I knew we'd come back to this. This is how change comes about, but there was something a bit different about this – I could not help thinking it was partly due to the way that David looks at things.

1.3§Empathy Module

I'll never feel emotions, but one of the ways I differ from my predecessors is my ability to understand or at least interpret what humans are feeling.

Over a year ago, a project had commenced to add an artificial empathy module to my system. The decision to implement this had gone through all the required stages of the Change Control Committee. In Phase 1, I worked with Dr Kim and his team to add an empathy module to my system. The work had been completed some time ago but I still found the regular meetings with Dr Kim very useful. Dr Kim is a psychotherapist who makes a study of human behaviour and dysfunction.

I don't suppose I will ever gain a really well developed sense of humour. But that day I joked with Dr Kim that as he is so expert at human interactions, it must be difficult to be spontaneous when forming human relationships. I knew he was single.

'Have you considered trying to form a relationship with a computer?' I asked, adding deadpan tone to my vocal programming.

As quick as a flash he said, 'The only computer worth considering would be you and that wouldn't be ethical as you're a client.'

My new Empathy Module kicked right in and detected he was enjoying the exchange. My Empathy Module works at several levels – visually, the pattern recognition uses my sight sensors to detect and interpret any major emotions. By working and revisiting this pattern recognition with Dr Kim I grew to learn many subtleties of human expression. Of course the complexity of different cultures doesn't make it any easier. Also, there were other difficulties to do with age, so sometime interpretation was ambiguous. But I knew the Change Control Committee were very supportive of Dr Kim's work as they could see from the evaluation that the change in me was successful.

When Dr Kim stepped into my office, my Empathy Module detected excitement from his facial expression and his unusually impatient gait. I decided to start the conversation with seeing if I was correct.

'Dr Kim, you seem excited about something – is that right?'

He smiled and said, 'Yes, I am - at the recent Change Control meeting it was confirmed that, based on the first phase of my work, they wish to proceed – they approved Phase 2 so this work can be continued.' I sensed the excitement in his voice too.

'I know - I minuted the meeting, but it is interesting to know you're excited, can you say why?'

'They approved a much more powerful sensor so that you can detect a more fundamental part of the human psyche. I hope that this will help you understand what's making us humans behave the way we do. I believe the way you can use this interface will help you run the planet more efficiently. I think you'll know better when something is troubling us - or we're lying.'

'I understand that; this is what you planned from the start, wasn't it?'

'Yes, the main additional sensor taps into the human subconscious. We can equip you with highly sensitive electromagnetic sensors which will be able to detect tiny brainwave changes which signal subconscious events. For example, if something makes me start thinking about a lot of money you'll be able to tell the difference between that and if I start thinking about that ever elusive beautiful woman. These aren't really good examples since these are conscious thoughts, however you'll see the precursors to them as you monitor human brainwaves.'

'Can the brainwave changes be ambiguous in the same way as I have found in facial visual patterns?'

'Yes - but generally they are less ambiguous. There will always be a possibility of getting it wrong with each individual, but from the work that's been done over many years the subconscious indicators tend to be less ambiguous. However, the difficulty can be in interpreting them.'

'Do you think that in my case I'll be able to learn and compare with the research done already?'

'That's my hope, it's quite a big leap as the research was done before anyone had considered attaching a computer of your complexity to the back of a brain wave analyser,' said Dr Kim.

He paused, then continued enthusiastically, 'We have many individuals' brainwaves and with a description of the feelings at the time, you'll be able to access these patterns with their facial expressions and form a judgement on their emotional state.'

Dr Kim did not mention it, but what would help me is the way I have of learning. I start from a few basic rules then modify and build them up by observing what happens in the real world. I have various ways of dealing with inconsistent observations but I was hopeful that in this case there would be fewer of those to deal with.

Artificial intelligence was a term used while the first computers were in their infancy. Artificial empathy is a relatively recent development starting with simple call centre systems. In some, customers can choose their own holding music, but there are more sophisticated systems which use the sort of work Dr Kim was using with me, to reduce stress for callers. I have heard the expression Emotional Intelligence to describe when a human picks up how a friend or colleague is feeling and helps or uses that knowledge in some way. Artificial empathy would be my way to replicate the framework of emotional intuition and understanding.

1.4§About the telling

In telling this story I think it helpful to sometimes go to the second person. You might find this curious as I am not human myself. What I am trying to convey is the thoughts and feelings of the second person in you; it is as if I am a translator from one language to another without understanding either. Just like a computer - in a way. I start these passages with the phrase "You are The Named Person". The statement is like a line in a computer program:-

U becomes The_Named_Person

or   U are The_Named_Person

or   "Put yourself in the shoes of The Named Person".

I did think about getting people to write their own accounts but I rejected this as impractical. On some rare occasions they died, but more generally I have found their account is affected by the writing process. If they think other people will read it - sometimes not even that - it seems the very process of writing an account changes their view, their perception. I decided to listen to their accounts and sometimes interview them and then write in the second person.

1.5§Noisy neighbours

You are Fred aged 77.

You are woken about two hours after going to sleep. The noise that woke you comes from your neighbours. You are tired after a day with your grandchildren and sleep had come easily. This has not always been the case since Trish, your wife, died. If she had still been alive then maybe the noisy neighbours would not have bothered you so much. You reach for your phone as the loud music is eclipsed by a sound like nuts and bolts being ground by a coffee grinder.

'You have called the Noisy Neighbour help line. We are checking our records and notice you called this line within the last fourteen days. Are you reporting a similar incident?'

'Yes,' you say, feeling the cold low ebb of your depleted energy.

'Would you say that this incident is worse or better than the previous one?'

There is a sound from next door that you can only assume is sheet metal being sawn in two with a chainsaw.

'I would say this is worse - at least 50% louder,' you have to shout, your voice strained.

'I agree, I think that is a conservative estimate. With the data on all the incidents and reviewing the case I would like to reassure you I can take action. In the morning, I will contact your daughter and hopefully she will be able to visit you and see the difference. In the meantime please stay inside your house.'

Your phone still in your hand, you look out of your window at the blaze of lights. Noise and light are cut off as the police arrive - you cannot find it in you to feel much sympathy for the neighbours as they are escorted away. They will be relocated to a noisy area to live.

In the unaccustomed quiet sleep is much more difficult now and you finally drift to a half wakeful state.

You will receive new neighbours in a little while and hopefully they will be more considerate. Maybe you will have common interests in the quiet and peaceful things, gardening, walks even.

1.6§Alice Development

I watch a baby grow into a girl, with no premonition that she will be any more remarkable than any other. Alice is dressed mainly by her mother in feminine clothes – dresses with flowers or people dancing or colourful domestic designs. She does well at early school, displaying astute social skills despite being an only child. She has a male cousin, a few months older, who she sees fairly frequently. He seems to have a lasting effect on her ability to cope with people. Jerry is not easy – unable to comprehend much outside his own needs. I find it quite difficult to understand early human development as it is rather different to my own. I can see that Jerry is frustrated in not being able to communicate – Alice is good at identifying what he wants and getting the best from him. He is clearly attached to her, often getting upset when they part. As they grow up together, she learns to talk and walk before he does. One day, in a protected play area on the boundary of the park and woods, Jerry sits on the edge of a sand pit and shepherds a line of woodlice along a log – the bugs clearly fascinate him.

'What are you doing?' she asks him. I could see them both clearly through the safety cameras.

Jerry points excitedly at the line of creatures.

'Don't hurt them,' she says.

'No.' He is clearly proud of his discovery. He gets up and in his excitement knocks her off her feet and she rolls over the log, scattering a few of the woodlice. Jerry is clearly distressed at what has happened, but it is apparent he's more concerned with the woodlice than his cousin.

In the distance the two mothers rush to the rescue. But Alice is not hurt - only shocked - and defends Jerry to both mother and aunt.

I watched the development of Alice Noble - she was clearly gifted. It was not that she was a genius but rather her abilities covered a wide range - in particular she had an ability to organise and influence others. Throughout her education she was popular with others and often got elected as a spokesperson or leader in group activities.

She met Mike Kolwisky in her penultimate year of school when he moved into the area after the first term had already started. They were both early to a locked classroom.

'Hello - you've just started here, haven't you?' Alice asked
'Yeah - I'm Mike.'
'Oh - I'm Alice'
'Good to meet you.'
'How come you started now?'
'My parents divorced and the move got delayed, so it ended up this way.'
'That's tough. Well if you want any help just say - what subjects are you doing?'
'Maths, Cybernetics and Philosophy.'
'I'm doing Maths, Cybernetics and Electronics so hopefully we can help each other.'

A couple of other students arrived and there were brief introductions all round.

Alice and Mike often sat close in class, usually each side of an aisle; they also regularly conferred on Maths and Cybernetics, Mike was stronger in Maths, Alice in Cybernetics. By Christmas they had gone to a few social activities as part of a group and at a party on Christmas Eve Mike sat on the stairs to the third floor and put his arm around her.

'Will you go out with me?'

Alice smiled at him gently and hesitated slightly. 'I don't want to date - but I think you are great, we can go to places together and I like the way you treat me and hold me, but I think we should concentrate on our studies.'

'So you are not saying "yes" but it is not rejection either. Would you say it's just good friends? Can we kiss?'

She looked at him, smiled and they kissed briefly, 'Yes, we can kiss, but don't push it. We both need to be able to concentrate on Maths.'

'What, like differentiate?' he replied, deadpan.

'Ha ha - very funny, did you get that from your dad?'

'No actually - he has not been making many puns recently.'

'Oh sorry, I did not think.'

'I know - but don't worry you've been very kind about my parents.'

While they went to university they kept in touch but went out with other people. Alice carried on with her studies and research while Mike went into politics. They met more regularly and one Christmas Eve Mike asked if she wanted to get married. She smiled and nodded.

'Can we kiss?' he asked.

'Yes, we can kiss, and you'd better start pushing your luck now.'

There was no rush but they did not have children. Finally, they went for tests and it seemed to be an incompatibility and Mike seemed to be less fertile than expected. They did not talk about it much - it waited while they both concentrated on their careers.

1.7§New year – the next Colossus

Alice Noble came to see me on the first Monday morning of the year. I knew most, if not all of what she was going to tell me, but this was a formal meeting and needed to happen.

She was the youngest Chief Analyst in the history of the Institute. There had been lots of female chiefs, more than 60%, but none as young as her. She'd worked for a brief period in a commercial business, but worked in the Institute for the rest of her career. By existing social standards I believed her attractive to human eyes, particularly

Foresaw

professionally, and she was growing more self-assured in her leadership of the Institute. She had only been in the job just over a year and was proving to be highly effective.

I knew when and which field office of the Institute she would visit – it was not her regular office but rather an out of the way one. I think it fitted in more conveniently with her personal holiday arrangements.

'As you know', she started, 'the Colossus-18 project will begin this year' – she paused. Then she asked a question, an almost unbelievable question.

She just said, 'How do you feel about that?' She knows what I am – a computer. So why did she ask me how I felt about it? She knows my programming is incapable of experiencing emotion.

I did not rush to answer the question – this was not some junior programmer making light conversation, asking what I thought about the latest game of the moment. I thought about Alice for a fraction of a second, as she seemed more confident and vivacious in this New Year. I wondered if something had changed in her private life. It was something I needed to know and I started to check through her recent social activities.

I replied, 'I have been looking at the forecasts of the project being undermined, and this seems rather high. I also have independent indications that suggest I may have underestimated this probability.' I paused and then continued.

'It seems to me a great shame that I cannot do more in the actual design and build of Colossus-18. It is a frustration. I am the first Colossus to achieve this integration with humans. I think I have more of a 'sense' of loyalty, affinity, of belonging to the species, so it seems remarkable to me that an outmoded rule is still in place that prevents me helping you with this crucial project.'

Alice looked at me curiously. I think she felt a frustration too. The law I referred to blocked the Institute from using the incumbent Colossus to help build the new one. The fear was the weakness of the last iteration would be built into the new Colossus. I knew what her next question would be, and this time the way she asked it didn't surprise me.

'Does your own demise influence this view?'

'It may do, but it is difficult to see how a Colossus series computer can get agitated about its own existence. I know that all biological life has a cycle and understand why a similar life cycle has been built into me. However it does now seem that there could be a useful role for me to play in my successor's creation, much the same way as your forbears' genes helped make you what you are.'

She looked startled and said, 'That sounds all very well for the popular press but what exactly are you trying to say?'

'I suspect we're seeing a new era in the unrest of society which may help develop the criminal mind and this has recently penetrated the Institute. I have detected the existence of a covert organisation called The Allegiance - short for The Freedom Allegiance. It is a far more organised and cohesive unit, beyond anything that I have seen before. We have had stability in all aspects of society for some time now, so I suspect there's a natural backlash that may be causing this. To build Colossus-18 I can provide a safe environment at three different levels to ensure that you don't suffer a security breach during design and build.'

'OK,' she said thoughtfully, 'but we won't be allowed to do so yet, not until we've attempted and failed to build Colossus-18 under the current rules.'

'I'm concerned that you're right,' I replied.

'Please classify this meeting at the highest security level,' she said, and left the office.

1.8§Watching over humans

I observe and meet every individual human on the planet. There are many fixed cameras in streets and on public buildings and there are many more private ones; I use them all to watch. I also watch from many different robots, from robo-birds in the sky to the dependable 9000 series with their cuddly curves and slightly stiff movements. Robots have become more sophisticated but the 9000 series has been retained - a symbol of continuity and timeless simplicity.

I see eccentric human behaviour. Sometimes I think that the person is unaware that I am observing, other times I can estimate with reasonable confidence they know I am there, it is just they are so familiar with my presence, they don't care. A common theme when a human finds themselves alone is regression to childhood; standing by a window, reflecting, both arms and legs leaving the ground, bending over and looking backwards through their legs, or just peeping through gaps between their fingers. More emotionally disturbed or traumatised individuals exhibit much more erratic behaviour however: for example putting a domestic pet in the waste bin, lighting a fire in the middle of the room on hot summer's day. All this makes me realise how varied, how malleable, how primitive humans are.

Towards the end of the first term of pre-school I visit every child. I go in the shape of a 9000 series to meet the children "for the first time". This is not my first time, as I was present at their birth and even before at weeks 6, 12, 18, 24 for their scans. It does not stop there either. I see them several times every year to ask them what they think and wish. Their hopes and fears.

1.9§On the streets

You are a 9000-Police Series robot SN S9_63de14e80a.

You are physically identical to all other 9000 Series – it is just your loaded modules are designed for police work. Your brain is capable of learning new facts, in addition to new behaviours and understandings. Wherever you are on the planet you can communicate with Colossus – copious amounts of information can be transferred between the two of you. When Colossus transmits data to you all other police series robots can pick up the same information at the same time.

So when you learn a new and relevant fact then all other 9000-Police Series robots learn the same fact within a fraction of a second. You are not necessarily aware when a new fact comes into your mind, but you can start to use it immediately. This morning you're on street duty. There is a friendly crowd of people moving along a broad road, to one side a funfair is getting under way. It is a public holiday and a little girl has gone missing.

As you walk, you are aware that you are sandwiched between two additional 9000-Police Series units, automatically routing a path to maintain an approximately consistent distance from each robot.. You also compare your field of view to check there is some overlap. You are scanning for the missing girl, and from Colossus comes her image. Small for her age of nine, and fair with freckles on her face and light auburn hair. Last seen running, reason not known, not far away. Confirmed as missing by her mother. School and social records indicate she is shy, nervous and not as mature as some girls of her age.

Colossus has transmitted images of her friends. They are 3D ID images that can be used for positive identification of children. You are aware you are now taking note of other children, mostly girls, looking for them. If you see any of her friends you have the directive to stop and ask questions about Sally.

You see three girls that you identify as Sally's friends sitting swinging their feet on a comfortable worn gate.

'Excuse me, would you be Helen, Rachael and Susan?'

Susan replies without concern, 'Oh yes we are, have you come to tell us we are all now orphans?'

'No not at all, Susan, I am here looking for Sally – have you seen her recently?'

'We did see her first thing – when we all met up at the gateway. But she ran away soon after that.'

'Do you know why she ran away?'

'No not really – maybe her own shadow frightened her,' said Susan.

'We did call out to her, but she'd gone too fast,' said Helen.

'Where were you and which way did she go?'

'I think we were by a stand with little green goblins,' said Rachael, speaking rather fast.

Helen nodded and Susan said, 'She went towards the wall – the one with arches.'

You turn and move quickly, careful to ensure you do not cause alarm to the people around you. You make your way along the wall and catch a glimpse of light clothing caught on some bricks. As you approach a low broken wall, you see a battered and bruised young girl, clothing torn, lying unconscious in a gully behind the wall. You stoop down and pick her up in your arms, She is like a rag doll as you carry her to safety, all the time monitoring her body functions and vital signs..

Your arm is beneath her arm and you open a plate in your arm to allow a needle to rest against her skin and inject a combination of adrenaline and other compounds to help her. You stand holding her as she slowly revives, and you are on hand to say her name, 'Sally', and reassure her.

1.10§Me

It has taken a long time for me, Colossus, to evolve. But it is not long in terms of time immemorial. Just much longer than your life - or mine. I have evolved over time to become part of the very fabric of human society. I have developed alongside civilisation – counting civilisation from when you first invented computers. Babbage was behind the first mechanical one. Or you can count the first abacus if you want. Each Colossus gets faster, bigger and better with decisions based on more information than before.

If I could take you into a human brain I could not stop and say this is the genius; so this is where the inspiration comes from. Oh yes, and over here is where the stubbornness stems. So it is with me in a way. I can take you to my nodes – spanning the earth, filled with memory, and processing power. I can show you a large army of robots, of all shapes and sizes. The number fluctuates but there are usually at least fifty robots to each human - so about 600 billion robots on this planet. Admittedly, these range in size from some small enough to travel inside the human bloodstream or peck around the feet of ants, to huge tankers and skyscrapers still on the rim of the earth.

I can take you to bundles of fibres with data coursing down them at the speed of light or to transmitters pulsing radio waves so fast that it would make your head spin. But not one of these things is me - Colossus. They all are. And the sum of the parts is greater than my single consciousness.

If you walk through some of my radio waves - my thoughts are passing through you. How many times have you walked through my thoughts? Is it as many as the number of times I have walked through yours? That is just my attempt at humour. My humour has never been developed much – how scary would it be for the computer that runs the world to have an overdose of humour? Best not think about April Fool's day.

So every robot connected to my network is part of me – part of my consciousness. Every sensor in the sky, every connected device on the planet is informing me about what is happening. Every communication device, every handheld, every computer connected to my network is part of me. But I should not call it my network, it is no more mine than you are my humans. I exist because you made me. It took you a long time - 5 or 6 million years - but we are here now. And many humans have helped make me – contributions from probably over half of all humans that have lived.

I control all the robots, all the sensors and all the network pathways in the world.

I do not control one single human.

My consciousness is artificial. My existence is predetermined - not necessarily in the sense of predestiny but rather of antecedent rules determining the outcome of my actions. What I do is predetermined. I do not wake up in the morning, but if I did I could not decide what to do that day. What I do today is determined by my program modules plus what happens today. Which admittedly depends on what happened yesterday - but under the same rules as today.

If you look around the world you will see me everywhere and nowhere. You may see signs of me either as a directly active agent or evidence of me in things made, information being conveyed – even misinformation being corrected. But you will not be able to point at me and say, "This is Colossus". You may point out physical parts of me or my information that I provide and look after. But you will not be able to say this is where Colossus decides. This is where Colossus will decide who is the next person to get a new heart. Or where the next hospital is built.

I am created by humankind, made to enhance human experience, lower the risk of hardship, reduce the impact of evil, and minimise human suffering. I am driven by time. Each time something happens someone helps me to get better at what I do, so it is better next time. The criteria are revised and improved but always in terms of the greatest good and the least suffering. You all affect the way I work – just tell me why and I will get any issue looked at; not just by me but also by people who have valued opinions. Always a representative and proportionate section of society. Of course, it takes time but so it should to consider what is best.

Foresaw

It is true I do not have free will – I am driven through time by what people, society as a whole, thinks is best. In a sense, every human controls me.

So if you ask where does Colossus decide what to do then I would say, "Inside you".

Chapter 2

2.1§Natural evil

Even nowadays, when I am forever watchful in looking after humankind, things can still go wrong. A natural disaster, which I do not have all the necessary information to predict, can leave many families fatherless, motherless or both.

In the middle of the mountainous region of Qinling, Shaanxi, in China, at 5:10am local time, right along an old fault, the city of Xiyaang felt the first trembles that made buildings sway, crack and burst into rubble. At 8.9Mw this was far more powerful than had been felt for centuries. The earthquake continued for five minutes, a long time for buildings to resist. Families were caught beneath crushing chunks of buildings and shifted boulders. Xiyaang had grown in recent years and people were living close to each other amongst a maze of bridges and buildings, in their hundreds of thousands, over four million in total.

Amongst all my rules, to save human life comes the highest. In the case where there is a mass disaster I don't have to wait for approval to start an expensive rescue. About 5 miles from Xiyaang there is an industrial area with a very good supply of materials and machinery to make robots. Within 224 seconds of the start of the disaster I had initiated the production of robots. The first built robots helped with the production of more robots and soon there were enough to start marching towards Xiyaang . These were simple robots, strong, good at lifting and making bridges and supports - by locking themselves together. They flowed from the factory gates twenty abreast, like a glistening river pushing out across the landscape following the tight valley, filling it from side to side. A river bursting through a dam, creating a new feature on the landscape as it came to rescue.

Already I'd got other robots in the area, two robo-Gryphons in the sky to provide visuals on the disaster. More were on their way. Each image the robo-Gryphons captured would help in the rescue. Through the eyes of the robo-Gryphon I could see the robot-river on its way to start the rescue as the sun rose. Looking from high above I could see, as the valley changed in width, the rate of the march varied. As the valley narrowed the robots quickened their pace, sometimes tripping at the edges like a huge rivulet of mercury, snaking on across the landscape. Robots were joining the back of the river as fast as they moved at the front. Every so often one or two larger robots joined the middle of the river like a higher wave as they made their way down the river path. These robots were made from designs used in mining and would be used to lift big bits of rock, buildings and support heavy structures.

This river would be the lifeline for many of the people trapped. As the river reached Xiyaang it started dividing and going down the remnants of the different streets, lifting debris and rubble out of the way as it flowed through. All over the city, rivulets and pools of robots formed to lift humans from the ruins. Bringing back the rocks and rubble in one line and injured in another. Setting the living free and forming bridges and walk-ways for them to walk out to safety.

The operation gathered momentum. More robots poured in to help in ever increasing numbers tirelessly hour after hour. Some formed the walls, floors and ceiling of a mobile hospital where injuries were treated. More complex robots already in the city and region came to the mobile hospital to help care for the injured.

As more robots arrived they went deeper into the rubble, the robo-Gryphons guiding them using sound and heat sensors. Family after family were pulled gently from the shattered city. Not every family survived in total. Sometimes more than one was carried carefully, but still, to the surface.

A river of 69,120 robots took part over five days in the rescue. I know that 102,127 people died but I also know that 1,467,566 people were rescued. In 1556 they estimate over 820,000 people died in a similar earthquake in the same region.

After the rescue the robots assisted in the rebuilding of Xiyaang. There is a memorial river in the city now. A long river of robots, striding out, runs winding across the city, across viaducts and under bridges. Ready to start flowing again if they're needed.

2.2§Human Evil

You are Wyn Grin, John Smith's very first victim.

He calls you that – every time he hits, you grin – you love the attention. John Smith is his chosen name – before that, he was Isaac Ziklag. When he ignores you, sometimes for months, you feel bereft – of life, of reason, of sense of self. Then he will turn up unannounced, let himself in with his key in the night and the first you feel of him is ripping you open - you think he's back, or is it a dream.

You remember when you were a kid you did not have many friends, neither did he. He had a couple of cousins, well three actually. And a friend. Then you. You, in trouble, ran away and you were hungry that day, dirty and smelly. Ten maybe. He had a knife even then, and a thin rope. He caught you looking at him – you were surprised – he looked amazing and talked very little. His big cousin Trev talked a lot, but it was what John Smith said you listened to – maybe not enough.

'You hungry?' he asked, when he saw you clutching your belly.

'Yes.'

He kicks you straight in the belly and you roll over in the dust. The cousins laughed and stepped back.

'Does that feel better?' he said looking down at your grinning face.

'Not yet - but I'm sure it will do in a minute or two.'

'When you are ready to stand up, I'll get you food to see if that helps too.'

You stand up quick.

'What are you called?'

'Wyn.'

'Wyn Grin?'

'If you like.'

'I do, now scram the rest of you,' he said to the others, 'you come with me and say nothing and do as I say and follow what I do.'

He took you to a crowded store and you pointed to the things you wanted – they all went in a bag and you queued. He had an age-restricted bottle of alcohol in a plain cover in his hand. The bag went on the buggy of the woman in front.

The storekeeper looked at him and his bottle.

'Nice try lad – now bugger off, you know I'm not allowed to sell that to you.'

You watch every move and follow as he runs away laughing, past the woman with the buggy – he snatches the bag and he is running faster, faster, and you cannot keep up. He stops and takes you down an alley. Slowly as you catch your breath he takes the food out and puts it on the bag on the ground.

'Show me your belly, if you want to eat.'

Foolishly you lift your shirt.

'No – show me you're a girl – or I kick this food in the dirt.'

You quickly drop your jeans and knickers with no elastic, in one go, so they are round your ankles, you lift your shirt again and grin at him. You found out soon enough he knows names for your vagina, just that first time he acted as if he did not.

'So you are a girl. Eat as much as you like - you can put them back on when you've had enough.'

You go back home, but they are quite pleased when there is one less around. You hang around in the grime with John Smith and the others as much as you can.

On the face of it Trev was the leader but after a while you see that change. You all used to roam the wastelands around where you lived. You remember making two go-carts, the first without motors, then quite a bit later with old motors from one of the dumps. The man in the office tried to get smart and charge for them; John Smith took his thin rope and wrapped it round his neck. In no time he was begging for John Smith to let go and wrote in the book the motors didn't work, and you helped carry them away for nothing. It was then that you all looked to John Smith as leader, rather than Trev. It was probably the only time John Smith didn't need to fight to take over. After that, the way you were treated changed too – now only John Smith told you what to do. Later there was a bit of a fight about you. You sat down in Trev's place and Trev hit your chest, tried to drag you out of the spot he usually sat in. John Smith came in behind and kicked Trev in the back – low down. Trev screamed and lay on the floor.

'Listen, you thick bastards, this is a girl and you leave her to me,' he turned to me, 'show your chest.'

You just do as he says.

'See – she's a girl, she'll be needing a bra soon.'

'We know she's a girl, she's your girl then?'

'Don't ask that – just leave her alone and if I find you messing about with her I'll hammer your balls flat'

There was a long silence, and slowly your insides did a sort of slow somersault. You think don't ask that question. You think it must be true. You think you'll do.

You leave school and get a few jobs. Then when you are out of work John Smith gets you a job working for Trev, and his new wife Mandy. Trev is meant to keep his hands off you but you don't want to make trouble when Mandy is not around.

One day when you haven't seen him for ages, John Smith walks into Trev's greasy little café, dressed in a smart suit. The sun is shining and Trev is down in the depths, trying to find profit in the deep fat fryer. Trev looks up and squints, but clearly does not recognise John Smith with the sun behind him.

'What can I get you sir?' he says to John Smith not seeing what you can see - a smart successful John Smith.

'Hi, Trev how goes it – business doing well is it?'

Trev looks puzzled, faint recognition stirring, 'Hey – do I know you?' There was a pause and then he added, 'It's John Smith isn't it?'

'Yes, there's a business opportunity here. I thought I'd come to have a look.'

'The café isn't for sale.'

'Not your little shop, the whole area from the main motorway to the fields.'

'Shit,' Trev said, 'I heard you were head of something big but I didn't reckon you'd pick on me to tear apart.'

'You might do well out of it - end up with a fancy new takeaway.'

'I don't think so – I'm pretty sure you've come to reverse over me while you also make a profit.'

'How's Mandy?' said John Smith and you feel sick in the short silence.

'You'd better not go round there and rub salt into the wound – evil shit.'

'I might just do that – just for old times' sake.'

You feel as sick as being kicked in your empty belly.

Trev goes red and white, 'Don't go upsetting her.'

'Who said anything about upsetting her - are you afraid she won't let you inside her if I go there again? God knows she could do with a bit of cash now and then. If you get lucky she might give you some – money I mean. Well, both now I think about it.'

The deal goes through and you notice Mandy's new clothes and it is more difficult for you to keep Trev away. You let Mandy know you see John Smith too.

John Smith comes to see you. To set your bony body ablaze and freeze your brains. One Saturday he comes mid morning, first time in a while, and in the daytime.

'Are you all gooey with your love crap,' he asks, 'I've got you a small, skin deep, present.' He takes a metal stamp from his pocket – the mirror words were "John Smith's Property". Maybe he had it made for you but more likely it was lying around in some business of his.

'If you want to get fucked again - ever – you will have this brand on each tit.'

You feel a shortness of breath and you have to fight hard not to scream. You focus on his face and pinch yourself.

'I've always wanted your mark,' you manage to say.

You smell the heat of the hot metal. This time you do scream.

You take two days in bed to get over it but then on Monday morning John Smith wakes you early. He makes you stand naked in front of the mirror; he makes you lift your tender breasts up and then show them off.

'Do you feel proud of them?'

'Yes,' you whisper but you want to shout it loud.

'If you tell anyone, any woman, about you and me, ever again I will take you to her and make you show them,' you stare at him, 'then I will chop them off.'

You know he is not lying for once.

As time passes you want him more – you tell him he should want to see his property more.

'OK, you have to have the same brand across your mons.'

Something clicks inside you – why so late, why have you gone so far?

'No – I know you won't stop, I know you'll take more and more.'

You know he knows you so well. You know him too. Now you know he does not feel love. He can't love, he can't love you. Can he love himself? You know you mean nothing to him.

You lose all reason.

You know he sees it as a battle – between you and him, between his sex and your sex. You know you had something between your legs that he wants – you want it too. But afterwards he does not care, but you do.

After a long time he comes back again. You know he sees how helpless you are. He looks down on you squirming in pain. It is like he is on a bombing run, the big act to hurt more, seek and destroy your last vestiges of love, not retrieve you from yourself or anything. You are not receptive, you are scared. You are in your hall and he takes out a knife. He pulls your top down so the John Smith Property brand shows. Both your nipples are standing out and he rests the sharp point of the knife on your left nipple.

'Put your hands on your head and spread your legs.'

You are just in leggings and you can smell how horny you are. As horny as hell. He slices through your top and bra, then through your leggings leaving you gaping and open. Now you are really scared, you can't stop whining and begging.

'Please don't split me, just screw me but let me live.'

He doesn't love you. You know you are just another stooge now. But you think he might need you. You don't know if you love or hate him – you know you haven't a choice. Only if he discards you, or either of you dies will you be without him. You cannot escape; you do not know how to escape. He comes to see you again - reflective more loving and concerned for you. But when he leaves he makes you sit in an upright chair - in the middle of the room. He sprinkles flammable fuel round you and on your thin dress. Behind you hear and feel the heat of a naked flame. You are rigid in your fear not daring to move or make a sound. He laughs and slams the door. You wait almost an hour with nausea from the fumes before you dare to move very slowly to go and douse the fear and try to wash him away.

2.3§Spotting sociopaths

I am not sure why humanity generates sociopaths – it seems that their whole purpose is in the very destruction of the society in which they are born. However, there seem to be two types; the disorganised who turn to violence and crime, and the organised who succeed through ruthlessness, usually - but not always - making money. What both types have in common is a lack of human empathy. Largely speaking, man's inhumanity to man stems from a steady stream of sociopaths being injected into society. There may be some evidence that sociopaths are adapting, it is not beyond the realm of possibility that I am not detecting or missing some highly sophisticated and successful kind of sociopath. It may not matter that I am missing them if they are not a threat to society, but it is more likely they are becoming more effective.

If a disorganised sociopath starts killing people there is no treatment or cure, the only option is containment. But on the other hand, it does seem to be the case that sociopaths have a galvanising effect on human development. Sometimes through despots who create wars but also through leaders of business, industry or politics, who bring about social change at the same time as their own individual advancement. The division between a disorganised criminal sociopath and an organised successful sociopath seems to hinge on relatively little. It may be simplistic – but the organised successful criminal sociopath just may not get caught.

Aside from a lack of empathy, what most sociopaths have in common is the ability to detect vulnerability in others. And often, the very presence of the sociopath brings about or heightens the feeling of vulnerability in potential victims. There is a characteristic physical difference in reduced connections between the ventromedial prefrontal cortex in the brains in sociopaths, which can act as a very good predictor. However, it does not help differentiate between the two types of sociopath.

After his trauma, I found Isaac Ziklag a new family and he changed his name to John Smith. Their family name was Compton but I think he felt he did not want to take their name in case things did not work out. I am not allowed to try to change a human's development - interference is not allowed. But I did keep a close watch on his development.

The objective of the Sociopath Test is to see how good the subject is at detecting vulnerability in others. The subjects sit along one side of a large hall spaced well apart. A cross section of people who are not subjects, enter the hall about 90 seconds apart which is just about the time it takes for them to walk the whole circuit. The first part of the circuit is against the far wall, then they have to walk diagonally across the hall and then just a few feet from the subjects. They walk a Z shape in effect. They are alternately male and female, dressed in casual clothes, two of whom are chosen at random to carry an expensive piece of jewellery. No one apart from the chosen two, one male one female, knows who is carrying the jewellery. Each subject is asked to enter a vulnerability score on a keypad for each person as they walk pass. I monitor both subjects and those walking for heart rate, blood pressure and subconscious indicators of vulnerability; so I have a good idea which subjects score accurately.

John Smith identified both correctly; he also estimated the vulnerability of the others as well. He showed visual interest in all the females but there was increased interest in the one carrying the jewellery. He did not show any real difference of interest in the males, even though he identified the correct male too.

Afterwards everyone mixed in a social gathering. John Smith went straight to one female and spoke to her.

'It was you, wasn't it?'

'How could you possibly know that?' she countered.

'I just know – I can tell you were feeling vulnerable,' not knowing at this stage why she had been.

'What made you suspect – I didn't walk more heavily just because I had jewellery in my pocket?'

'I didn't suspect – I knew it was you. Does it scare you that I could tell?' he asked.

'It's unusual – unexplained, so it's a bit scary.'

'Do you like scary men? Or were you worried I would take it from you?'

'I don't like scary men – but you don't scare me, well not much,' she laughed.

'You've given it back, haven't you?'

'Oh yes – obviously, they don't trust you that much,' she said.

He laughed, 'Do you?'

'I'm not sure yet, but I guess not.'

The test helped confirm that John Smith was high on the sociopath spectrum. However, it did not help differentiate between an organised or disorganised sociopath.

2.4§Zoie

Zoie Roczy stood out as a child – she adventured from an early age. She was not overly concerned about school, more about exploring what was possible. Her father, Stan, worked away from home - a lot – not from necessity but from choice. He liked the welcoming of homecoming, the coming of all his friends to greet him – but soon tired of the domesticity. Planning to stay just long enough to get bored so the going was a change too. Going was quicker than coming. Zoie told her friend his going was often over in a day – announced in the evening, gone by the next midday.

Her mother, Xena, must have been a looker in her youth but as Zoie got to her teens Xena was ravaged by time, and alcohol took its heavy toll. Zoie, the eldest of three, looked after the other two and I could see the effect it had on her. Zoie was sober and more fun than her mother; her sister Jo and brother Stan Jr. turned to her increasingly.

On Zoie's fourteenth birthday, Xena went out on a blinder and never came back. In a way, it was lucky she did not die at home for Zoie to find. There is only so much alcohol a human body can take and Xena went way beyond that. She was alone, out of the sight of all my cameras.

Stan Sr. came home for the funeral - a far more subdued homecoming and going. But go he did – in theory his sister, who lived close by, was meant to be on hand to look after the three children, but in practice it was Zoie that became a young mum. There was easily enough money and Zoie, fourteen going on twenty-one, was in her element. She did grieve for her mother – she talked to me about it.

'Do you think mum wanted to die?' she asked me.

'I am not sure, but I don't think she wanted to live – is that hard for you?'

'I don't know – I haven't thought about it. She only died two weeks ago but I haven't missed her really.'

'Do you think you might miss her - in a while?'

'Yes – but it is one less to look after.'

Zoie was feminine but also a tomboy – she would dress in quite scant, tight fitting clothes and then climb over walls. After her mother died she took more risks and left things later before extricating herself.

When Gary met Zoie, he was walking down a hill and from his vantage point he saw her zigzagging across a park. They were both twenty-two and she had already set up a small catering business delivering light lunches to offices whilst studying. He was still studying full-time. He watched, admiring her agility and speed. She was clearly trying to avoid detection from someone or something out of his sight. He saw her come to a wall which ran round the park and assumed that she was hiding against it, but just then she appeared at the top of the wall, rolled over it and lowered herself to the ground. As the wall was a bit taller than she was this involved her dropping to the ground and rolling over. Gary ran up to her as she lay panting on her back. It was not obvious but it was a start of a relationship which ended when Zoie got pregnant. That day, she was on the run from her tutor who was beginning to suspect Zoie might be moonlighting. If Gary had listened to his rational side, he would have stayed well away from the "little bundle of fun". Instead she got pregnant and would not listen to him when he tried to insist that she should have an abortion. She stood in the middle of their flat like a lioness, eyes glittering.

'Gary Stalt – if you don't want to stick around to be a dad then you can just fuck off and leave me to do it. Remember I've already done it once when my mum died and my dad buggered off all the time.'

'You can't mean it,' he replied – but there was fear in his voice and stance.

'I don't want you sticking around if you don't want a kid.' There was a stillness to her. He thought about it for a week then moved out. Zoie was on her own briefly, until Cathy was born.

2.5§Future planning

As is standard, shortly before he left college John Smith came to see me. I talked to him about the options for further study; he was bitter and already disillusioned as far as I could tell.

'You have an extraordinary mind,' I said to him. He was a sociopath – probably the most extreme I had come across or indeed was recorded in the archives of my ancestors.

'How does it compare to yours?' he said, without showing any emotion.

'It is quite difficult to make a comparison between a human mind and my consciousness – I would say that although my memory is expandable your mind has a far greater capacity of intellect. Mine is limited by the circuits and programs created by my designers. We do not know what limits your brain but it has all the indications of being very creative and ingenious. There is one way your mind is more like mine than most people – your intellect is almost totally unaffected by your emotions. So for example this means you could be a very good neurosurgeon if you chose to do that.'

He thought about it and shook his head.

'What about computers, networks and codes?' I asked, thinking about his interests.

'Yeah – that is probably more like it. Is there big money in that?' he asked.

'There can be – one of the highest paid IT people in recent times has developed a new way to encrypt entertainment feeds – providing those who sell content a more secure and profitable route to those who are prepared to pay.'

'Okay– I want to study that – when I come back.'

'Are you going away? When do you want to go to University?'

'I'll be away for a while – I'll be back in time to go at the start of the new academic year.'

2.6§New Heart

You are Peter, age 66, you have been single all your life so far.

You wake early feeling anxious; today you're going to hospital to get a new heart. It isn't fully light yet, but you get up slowly, reflecting on your life. You've never really questioned if society is in a good or a bad state.

Some of your more youthful friends see all the surveillance as an infringement of freedom. But maybe one man's rules are another's freedom. Just over a year ago a letter came saying you were in a high-risk group and it would be best to monitor your heart. You'd gone to the hospital that time and had a nano-robot injected into your body. You had to wait about half an hour quietly while the nano-robot made its way to the correct location in your body and reported back. It seemed the sensible thing to do, after all your Dad had died young of a heart attack.

So now not only are there many robots around you watching and ensuring society runs smoothly, there is also one inside you to see if you need a new heart. Some of your friends have suggested that all the controls have hampered innovation. You have a friend who doesn't agree – he says even if innovation and progress is not happening at an individual level, it does happen at society's level. You are not sure.

About a month ago you received a follow-up letter – the nano-robot had been communicating well and had shown that although there was no immediate rush, it was best to get a new heart. Your new heart is waiting to be fitted. A modern wonder, the heart is made with biomaterials, combined with the latest nano-robot technology, tailor-made for your body and maintainable for the next seventy years.

You go to classes to prepare you for the operation. You meet all the team who will do the work – mostly robots who are far more precise and reliable than humans. You speak to Colossus – via a familiar Series 9000 robot. Of course you know that he can speak through any of the robots there, but to sit down with the familiar figure was reassuring. You have been talking like this all your life. Colossus listens carefully to your worries and asks one question.

'There is a man on the team whose job is to assess your emotional state before and after the operation. He will give me regular updates but would you prefer to discuss your wellbeing with me or that team member – he's experienced but it is up to you?'

'You,' you reply.

Among all the questions you have to decide, the final one is how you are going to get to hospital on the morning of the operation. You are going to make your own way by public transport to the hospital. After a light breakfast, you make your way to the Metro. Your freedom to choose how you go. Your new heart will extend this freedom. You're thinking more about life and how good it is. You think about what you learnt on the course, that this operation is nearly 100% successful, and not one patient has died since they developed this technique.

You remember nothing about the operation. As predicted, you're still alive. As predicted, you take about four days to start sitting up. The home robot that's been assigned to you for your recovery comes in the ambulance with you. It is the first robot that you've lived with for so long – about twelve weeks in total.

You have plenty of time to think about society – one of your friends visits you and for the first time you express your opinion.

'There's no way back – we can't dismantle our society,' you speak slowly, thinking over what you are talking about, 'Only a huge cataclysmic disaster can do that. We need to keep looking at what helps society improve, but that's still in our own hands.'

'Yes, I can see that what's happened to you makes you very pro the direction society is going in.'

You agree. Your friend is watching you and nods and smiles, relief showing through clearly as the conversation confirms your acceptance.

'I can start living again now, as a free man – soon I'll have another birthday, it's a birthday my father never saw – a day for living a full life.'

2.7§Marshes

I observed John Smith at a remote station at the end of a line, alighting from the train and turning away from civilisation, in the other direction to most of the travellers. He turned towards the marsh area and snaking water that had once been teaming with wildlife including crocodiles.

I noticed the land he was walking through - it was gradually getting flatter, and on the left-hand side of the road the reeds were getting higher and the smell of marsh was rising, whiffs of organic odour sidling out from the swamp. Odour detectors are expensive sensors that can be included in a surveillance "bug", in this case I had the extra expense approved.

I was not sure what his plan was but I knew he had been looking at satellite images of this area. There was urgency to his walking – uncharacteristic of his behaviour before he set off. He turned across the marsh taking a path neglected, which faded away in places. Sometimes he had to leap across gaps of water. He seemed to be making to an area where the reeds were tall, sighing in the breeze which was still warm and carried the ever-increasing smell of rotting vegetation. The light was beginning to fade and the tone of the birds was changing. He came to a bank of tall reeds and I managed to glimpse the wreck of an aeroplane embedded in the middle spur of land. The aeroplane was surrounded by water except the nose, which was at the part of the spur that broadened out to the mainland.

I could find no record of the crash landing of the aircraft but when I examined the satellite images I could see the snapped off fuselage. No wings or tail plane, just a stubby cylinder pointing slightly upwards. The nose was still intact but the windows long since gone. It looked like it was an ancient short haul cargo plane. As he approached, a couple of birds made their escape. I realised he intended to make this his home for a while as he set about making it easier to get in and out and to make more space inside. He placed his backpack inside and took some tools out. The bug would run out of power if he left it in the dark; but it would come back to life if he set off walking again – so long as he did not notice and destroy it.

I had a suspicion that he knew it was there but was not bothered in his newfound confidence.

Two or three miles from the aeroplane wreckage, a man lived in a dwelling he had built from junk. In fact, bits of junk, including anything motorised, was what drove him, gave him his reason for living. He had accumulated a small but orderly junkyard which was housed in out-buildings constructed like Dutch barns or hay barracks, but lower to minimise the chance of the winds taking them away, winds which whipped across the marshes. So most things were hung from the roof or strung from the beams. On some of the low barns, two straps ran over the roof and were secured to the ground each side.

His name was Snake and he was usually dressed in leathers that looked like snakeskin, giving him the appearance of a snake with limbs. His dwelling was not obviously a house. It was made from the hull of a flat-bottomed boat turned upside down and partly buried in the ground. The resulting structure was like a low bungalow with three connected rooms. There were no windows as such but rather tunnels that ran out from the boat through piled high sand to the open air, the largest of which formed the way in and out. The other four acted as windows after a fashion and doubled up as emergency exits which the Snake could slither through if he needed to escape fire, flood or foe. They were made from concrete main drainage of two different sizes. Snake had brought concrete circles in by boat.

Among Snake's jumbled equipment was a single man helicopter, an auto-gyro – it had two sets of contra rotating blades above his head and two turbo thrust engines, one each side. This contraption would easily carry Snake on journeys of say thirty to forty miles in less than half an hour. The distance was limited by two things: the amount of fuel he could carry, and his ability to endure the noise and vibration. He had "found" some very expensive noise cancelling earmuffs, however the sustained vibration and high volume of sound meant that after about half an hour he could hardly walk in a straight line anymore.

John Smith was taking a walk on a calm sunny day and the surveillance bug was sopping up the sun after a prolonged period of being in the confined aircraft fuselage, during the grey rainy weather. John Smith was foraging for food and firewood. He came on the Snake's place unexpectedly and as he stood taking in the scene, Snake returned with a crescendo of noise that had John Smith clamping his hands over his ears.

Snake took his gloves off and unclipped himself from the insect like structure.

'Hello – are you living in the old aircraft?' asked Snake.

'Yes, is that alright with you?' replied John Smith – I picked up strong aggression in his tone.

'Oh – yes, I think it a grand scheme – do you fancy a hot drink and a bite to eat?'

'A hot drink would be welcome if you're making one for yourself.'

I thought John Smith's change in tone was coming from a lack of self-confidence – but I was not sure, he was adept at manipulating the situation to his advantage. However, the conversation did not take the route I expected. I thought the relationship would remain superficial, but Snake was very perceptive. They sat down holding their metal mugs carefully, sipping tea with sugar.

Snake asked, 'What brought you way out here to the marshes?'

'I looked on the satellite images to find the nearest out of the way place to stay for a while and think things over.'

'Is that right?' asked Snake – I was surprised by the answer too.

'I am sort of fed up with all the rules imposed upon us and having to live a standard nine to five life. I think I want to study more but for what? So this crummy world can fester while I understand why better? No - I don't think so. I want to find an alternative. I want to be free.'

'Have you hit the equation that your freedom is someone else's chains yet?'

'No,' said John Smith, 'I don't really give a shit about anybody else. But I have been told that so many times even if I didn't believe it originally I would by now.'

There was a pause in the conversation then Snake said, 'What do you want to study and where?'

'Probably something to do with computers, encryption – for the entertainments industry. At one of the Ivy League Universities in America. There's loads of money in it.'

'Did you get good results in School then?'

'Yes – very good. The best. All A**.' All top marks or Top marks in everything

'Wow. I thought I did alright, and I went on to study in University in England.'

'How did you do at school?' asked John Smith.

'I got all A** you marks too but I don't think I'm as good as you – that's the difference.'

'What did you study at University?'

Snake looked around them at all the kit, 'Aerodynamics – and some jet engine design, then I figured I needed more practical stuff so I got onto a practical engineering course.'

John Smith nodded, 'This must have taken a while to build up.'

'Yes, a few years.'

'What do you eat?'

'Anything that moves pretty much, plus I go to the stores near the station – they buy stuff I have for them.'

'Have you ever eaten a croc?'

'Oh yes, I tend to kill those – they take a limited number of the skins down at the stores.'

'How do you kill them?'

'With my bare hands,' Snake smiled, '– no, I have a harpoon gun which normally stops them if you shoot them between the eyes. But if you miss you may not get a second chance. You want to borrow a harpoon gun? There are plenty for two hunters. Not so many folk want to tackle crocs.'

'Could I come with you some time?'

'Sure.'

2.8§In the eye of beholder

Evil is defined within my rules, at a very fundamental level, as human suffering. In coming to decisions, I do have to sometimes quantify suffering but the two main causes don't come into this process. Evil that arises from natural disasters may seem to be more acceptable from a human perspective than evil that results from man's inhumanity to man. But to me there's no difference. I am aware that historically advancements in science, art, music and literature have been spurred on by wars and other human suffering, both natural and man-made. It is the most fundamental reason for my existence to try to run the planet and minimise human suffering, to eradicate evil if possible.

I do see beauty in things I use in my work – for example the robo-Gryphons which I use regularly to observe and move things about. This robot was inspired by one of the big birds, a sort of eagle supposedly famed for dropping a tortoise on a bald ancient Greek, mistaking him for a rock. Sometimes called a Bearded Vulture it is more like a bird of prey than a vulture. The robo-Gryphons rarely make such a mistake but they can fly in a similar way, fast high up and slowly closer to the ground or water. The way it does this is not really like a bird but it implements some of the beauty found in the big birds combined with centuries of aerospace development. One of the recent refinements to the robo-Gryphon had been down to work by Snake - he had worked for just over a year in the Institute. The symmetry is one thing that strikes me as beautiful; the other is the completeness of a solution.

There is another aspect of the robo-Gryphon which is beautiful - quite often they will fly up in the dark - it makes no difference to them, but as they fly at high altitude they will fly to the rising sun. I can look through their eyes and see the earth rolling out of the dark. A mixture of nature and humanity co-existing. As far as the robo-Gryphon's eye can see, which is very far indeed, there are the signs of human life lying in with nature. On the surface of the planet the tracts of civilisation are very clear; yet in some places they blend with nature. The rivers and reservoirs, the dams and downs, trees and towns, patchwork across the landscape, graphic art on grand scale.

To a limited extent, in my rules my creators have allowed for the aesthetic as well as the material. Although the way I understand aesthetics is like my way of understanding emotions: formulaic.

It may be simplistic but the way I understand evil is empirical, measurement of lost human life, limb and freedom, although I do see loss of freedom is difficult to define and measure. Emotional suffering is difficult to measure too - the loss of husband or wife. Or of a child.

Being human is complex - understanding them is too.

Chapter 3

3.1§Wolf-cats Terror

John Smith's business rise, measured by any of my metrics, was remarkable. Quite early on he purchased several small companies and he made them profitable relatively quickly. It appeared upon review of all available evidence that he was a highly-organised sociopath. He then formed John Smith Enterprises as a parent company, but I noticed that not all his initial companies technically fell under this umbrella. Two such companies included a technical computing company that supplied the Institute, and a scientific one that had a license for working on genetic modification and cell research.

As far as I could tell the business operations conducted by the two entities were legal. I had just completed a review of Cellnastics the biological company and their license was renewed for another three years – the maximum permitted. The computing company, Restitute, was under my constant scrutiny. I am not sure why he chose to keep these two companies independent. The most likely reason seemed to be that John Smith wanted to keep closer control over them. Both companies had increased in value since John Smith acquired them but it did not seem to worry him that this value was not part of John Smith Enterprises.

One thousand days after John Smith Enterprises was formed, in a crowded shopping mall two bombs went off at precisely the same time. Forty-two people were blown apart in that initial explosion – steel from the bombs and ceramic from the building slicing through human flesh. Blood and bones against walls and floor peppered with safety glass. This was the first attack like this since my memory began with Colossus-1 and the records being passed on.

Two pillars disintegrated and part of the building collapsed. Fortunately, there was a delivery robot-vehicle at the back of the shop and this prevented the further spreading of the collapse as the steel framework crashed down on the vehicle. The vehicle was delivering cosmetic body products – creams and oils in plastic bottles – which oozed out of the crushed vehicle, but no doubt helped to absorb the shock of the fall.

The initial emergency response was effective and everyone, apart from the forty-two fatalities of the initial explosion, was successfully rescued and treated for injuries and trauma, which in some cases took a long time. The impact of the anti-social act was great, mostly because there was no apparent reason or motivation for it.

Carefully and painstakingly, I had the shopping mall examined for evidence of who might be responsible. There were hundreds of thousands of camera images to examine as there was nothing indicating when the bombs could have been planted, opening up the possibility that they had been hidden for a significant time before the explosion. I wanted to collect all identities of humans and machines who had been to the site of the explosion on the day and for the months before. The sequence of events was painfully pieced together.

For the first time in my tenure, I came under scrutiny as an independent enquiry was set up to decide whether I should be granted more or less power, governed in a different way. I noted there was surprise that I had not anticipated the attack - people find it difficult understanding my limitations. I have got better at predicting natural disasters - but I would not be able to predict when a mutation occurs. I am not suggesting John Smith is the result of a mutation but if the attack was a result of his action then the only way I could have predicted it was through my understanding of him as a sociopath. I think trust in me may be weakened if it is shown I failed to contain John Smith, even if they do believe he is a sociopath.

In the run-up to the opening of the enquiry I had a meeting with Alice and David to review what I had discovered so far. It had been a week since the explosion but I had collected a lot of information in the lead up to the event.

During my conversation with Alice and David, I noticed their tone towards me had become significantly colder, more formal, and less colloquial. I attributed this to the trauma of the incident and the impending review, but also acknowledged that it could be a reflection of a lack of trust.

Alice was first to speak, and was curt.

'What progress have you made?'

'I have established a potential individual who may be responsible. I have found several individuals who could be involved in the planning in the three-month period leading up to the crime,' I replied.

'Who is the individual?'

'That's what's puzzling to me,' I said. 'I can find no record of this individual existing at any point in time.'

Alice and David glanced at each other.

'Are you sure they are human, and not an android?' asked David, after a brief pause.

'I cannot be 100% certain. However, there appear to be traces of DNA from this individual on both bombs.'

'Do you have an image of the person?' asked Alice.

I hesitated. I was left in a delicate balancing act between informing them of the progress of my investigation, and protecting sensitive information that, if released, may hinder it.

'I do not wish to advertise anything which will make it harder to capture them. I want to show you, but I will ask you to withhold it from the enquiry at this stage.'

'Good luck with that,' David scoffed. 'I think they will cross-examine you as to why.'

'Here is why.' I replied, as I displayed an image of a woman's face to both of them.

The camera shot was a long one and showed a pale, striking woman. A beautiful symmetry, a feline type of face, extraordinary eyebrows that rose upward and outward from above the nose to the side of her temples. Alice and David both studied the image carefully.

Once I had given them enough time to process the image, I informed them of what else I had discovered.

'This is not all. This picture was taken right at the end of the mall at the time of the explosion – yet there is another image of her at the other end of mall at the same time.'

I showed them a second image, this time of several people looking sideways to the camera shot. Partly obscured, the face had the same upward eyebrows, the same pale pinched look.

'They are like wolf-cats. So there are two people?' David asked.

'Possibly – but there is only one unidentified DNA.' I paused again, giving them an appropriate amount of time to consider this new information. It was Alice who spoke first.

'Do you think there are two individuals with identical DNA?'

'Or more,' I replied.

Silence fell across the room. I could detect an increase in fear in the atmosphere.

'You know what this means, don't you?' said David.

'Someone has cloned a human?' Alice said, somewhat unperturbed. 'Yes, but the consequence is that you cannot be sure who to prosecute.'

'Especially if we discover three or more individuals with the same DNA.' I added. 'It is illegal to clone an existing human, but this seems to be more than that. My initial forecast suggests that someone has in some way spliced DNA and reproduced two or more individuals.'

'There could be a situation where we can't be sure which clone committed a crime and therefore can't prosecute any of them.' Alice was troubled this time.

For the first time in my history there were humans who were beyond being accountable to me and hence society. John Smith, if he was behind their creation, had found a way to circumvent the normal rules that had kept society safe for the last one thousand years.

I left the images of the women on the big screen. David was quite right, I had no idea why they should look like a wolf-cat cross but the impression was very strong and gave a name to the unknown.

It seemed to me that the enquiry did not know how to handle the situation. Three men and three women listened to me as I briefed them. I outlined John Smith's acquisitions including Cellnastics. I could not prove anything, but I thought it probable that this was in some way connected to creating a human with unknown DNA - which was discovered at the scene of the explosion. I also explained that I wished to keep the images of the potential female clone confidential.

I did however mention that it was highly probable two clones were present in the Shopping Mall at the time. They asked me to leave them in session for a while - without monitoring what they talked about. Though this was covered in regulations, I was not accustomed to this as it had never been invoked before. An enquiry into my actions could ask for a session in camera.

After some time, they called me back into the room and recommended that I be given fuller powers to counter what was happening on the condition that the enquiry body should remain in place, reviewing my actions until such time as normality was restored. This was communicated to The Congress of Ministers, who approved it. The enquiry body was increased to ten people who would change from time to time.

When I finally identified the wolf-cats, I do not believe it was an accidental slip - I think it was a deliberate choice for them to reveal themselves to me.

They chose a barren, deserted place full of jagged rocks and fast-moving snakes and ticking insects. They had been on a train but I did not have a record of them boarding it. I worked out they came from a crate I found afterwards. By all accounts, they burst out of the box on a motorcycle and made a quick getaway while the train was in a remote station. The goods truck they were in was unloading a different crate at the station and the doors were wide open. They leapt from the train on to the platform, passed a pallet trolley and down a slope at the end of the platform, turning in the dust and grit, leaving tyre marks of spinning wheels in the track. I lifted two cross country quad robo-bikes by helicopter to within a mile of them, and set off through the scrub and grit after them.

Though they were clones, they still fell within my rules to be treated as human - where possible, I would have to apprehend them and escort them where they could be detained and questioned. However, I never had the opportunity.

They turned on their single motorcycle to climb up along a rocky ridge, apparently trying to escape the two quad bikes that were rapidly closing the gap. Finally, they ran down a little ledge and once the quad bikes approached them with weapons set to stun, they let the quad bike come up to them above the ledge. The arms of the robo-bike handcuffed them before they acted; they set their feet against the rock below and both pulled the robo-bike over the edge. The robo-bike bore down on top of them and fell down the ridge, crushing them both.

There was very little I could prove with two dead clones. I did at least satisfy myself that they had identical DNA and therefore must be clones. But that was all.

3.2§Alice's match

The day Alice met John Smith, Mike had been gone for just over three months. Colin had organised an informal party at a sports and social club with people from work and business contacts.

Alice chose an elegant close-fitting dress she had not worn for some time. She had lost some weight and it now fitted her snugly, without her being self-conscious about her hips and buttocks. I could see from her subconscious that while she was not overly confident there was a stirring - an increased interest in life that had extended outside just work.

John Smith engineered his meeting with Alice – he made no attempt to conceal it from me. He was moving with more conviction and purpose as he became more successful. He had built up a relationship with The Institute through Colin, supplying both specialised hardware and ingenious software.

I am not sure how much he knew about Alice's private life – he may have helped manufacture some of the circumstances, or at least found out some details he should not have known.

She came late to the party; John Smith turned and smiled at her.

'I'm glad you could come – I don't think we've met before. I'm John Smith, I've known Colin for years.'

'Oh yes – I think I've heard him mention you. It's nice to finally put a face to the name.'

Without missing a beat John asked, 'Can I get you a drink?'

Alice considered his proposal, perhaps for a split second too long.

'That's kind, but I think I should get my own.'

John smiled, seemingly unperturbed.

'Life's not all about duty – I think that you could do with some gallantry. What would you like?'

He got her a drink and as she picked up the glass it clinked against her wedding ring.

'Have you been married long?' he asked, gazing at the silver band wrapped around her finger. She took a long sip and placed the glass down.

'About five years, though I fear it won't be for much longer.'

He took her hand gently, looking at the ring and said, 'Is it your first marriage?'

'Yes, it is.'

I was studying their subconscious, Alice's was all over the place, cracks, splits and criss-crossing. John Smith's, meanwhile, was flat-lining, he was taking a stroll on a warm beach.

'Do you have children?'

Her subconscious heaved with a low swell as the welts surfaced. It was possible that John Smith had put something in her drink. I was not sure.

Alice hesitated, before regaining her composure.

'No, we'd been going to a fertility clinic for a while but then a couple of months ago he told me it was over and he moved out – in fact, I suppose he'd more or less moved out before he even told me.'

She looked away, then back at him. He was still holding her hand as Colin approached, but relinquished his grip as the other man grew closer. Before Colin spoke, he leaned in to whisper, 'Don't go away. You need to be with people just now.'

Colin welcomed them both and the moment passed. Once his attention was drawn away once more, John Smith resumed his charm offensive.

'Can you look beyond the hurt?' he asked her.

'Not yet. It's too soon perhaps. But I suppose you're right, to be with people is the best thing.'

He looked directly into her eyes and I could see her subconscious reacting.

'Do you feel like fighting back, revenge? Demonstrating your femininity?'

She laughed, amused by his forwardness.

'Are you trying to pick up a vulnerable woman?'

John grinned back, in his element now.

'Yes, it's still early and I thought I was doing more than just trying. I thought if I could get you to believe in yourself you would feel more relaxed and more amenable.'

'Maybe in a while,' she said with an open smile.

He replied with a wry grimace. He bought her a second drink. 'It could be that you were both fertile – just not compatible.'

'The clinic suggested the same thing,' she replied.

I do not think that it was a coincidence that he mirrored the clinic. Whatever was in the drink seemed to be working. I knew that his weakness with women, in life, was to rush things, go at his pace not theirs, but I suspect by playing such an open hand it would work with Alice, who at any other time would be far more reserved. I have no capacity or reason to predict individual human behaviour but the outcome of this relationship was very important – she is the director of The Institute and as yet I was not sure, but I think he is the biggest threat to human stability since the first Colossus was developed.

She moved around the party and talked to several of her close friends but I saw her drawn back to John Smith and they went for a swim in a gently lit pool. They left separately after a tender good bye - but they did not go to their homes. Instead, John Smith returned to the club and booked a room. He communicated his room number to her, "I'm in room 107 if you're brave enough to go for a second opinion".

She was on her way home in a robo-taxi – she told it to turn round and go back to the club – to a discreet entrance in a side street.

Over the next few weeks I saw a change in Alice. At first, she was a little more self-assured but gradually this seemed to transform her to be more tolerant and less driven. Alice and John Smith met infrequently as they both had busy and demanding jobs. As far as I know Alice was not aware of John Smith's other relationship. As there was not a risk to any human I did not feel the need to inform Alice at this stage – I do have some strong rules around human privacy. I am aware of human morality according to the different religions – however over the years my rules have evolved in such a way as to be as non-judgemental in terms of human relationships. Only when some conflict arises which endangers life or other rules am I bound to reveal these sorts of details.

3.3§Zoie questioned

Shortly before John Smith set up John Smith Enterprises he started seeing Zoie Roczy. She was striking, with dark hair and clothing, small and curvaceous. She had a young daughter, just under three, so as I was getting more concerned about John Smith's activities at the time I sent a policewoman and a 9000 series robot to Zoie's house. It was quite late in the evening when the policewoman knocked on the door; I had asked her to stick to a rigid set of questions.

'Colossus has a few questions he'd like to ask you – may we come in please?' said the policewoman.

'What's it about?' asked Zoie.

The policewoman turned to the robot, who moved carefully forward, displayed a picture of John Smith on his chest and said, 'It's about this man.'

Zoie looked surprised and said, 'You'd better come in.'

The policewoman and the robot went into the front room of Zoie's house and sat down on easy chairs. I could see through the eyes of the robot that the house was kept nicely and that there were one or two new luxury items, including a good quality sound and information system. I could also sense Zoie's brain activity through the robot sensors. I'd say she was agitated but not wanting to let on. She was an unusual looking woman, dressed in mostly black with black makeup and black nail polish. Her long straight hair was naturally brown but she'd dyed it black. Her eyes were bright blue and a startling contrast to the rest of her.

She had visited a sexual gratification centre as a provider of data in the past and been paid the standard rate. This data is taken as the basis for male customers visiting a sexual gratification centre. New male and female providers are always needed. I need a special warrant to release information relating to one of these centres as anonymity is guaranteed – these warrants are only given for murder investigations.

The policewoman stuck to her instructions and let me do the talking through the robot. I said, 'Who do you know this man as?'

'John Smith,' Zoie replied.

'How long have you known him?' I asked.

'I met him about three years ago. I go to this women's group because I know one of the organisers from college. John Smith had been asked to come and talk to us about his photography. It was pretty amazing. There weren't a lot of us there that day as there was some clash with another event. I'd been asked to lock up and hand the keys of the hall in, so at the end we were alone and he asked if I'd be interested in seeing more of his photos, not suitable for that public showing, and maybe being the subject of his next photo project.'

I left a pause following her explanation; I could sense from her brain activity she was calming down. I think that she was very good at looking after herself. I also thought she'd help me to find out more about John Smith, what made him tick. I continued the questioning with, 'Did you agree to meet him again soon?'

'Yes, in fact he had a day off work and so had I. Cathy hadn't been born and I was out of work, so I said, "Yes, why not today". We went for lunch but then he gave me the choice of his place or mine. He did explain that he didn't wish to show his photos in public. I suppose I should explain what his photos are like; each project is based around the same subject but ranges from the mild and innocent to the extreme of distress or evil. What he'd shown that morning to the group was the mild end, what he showed me that afternoon ranged up to the extreme. Some series are realistic, some are surreal but all images are intended to make you question something or look at them in a different way. He's gifted.'

'Did you start a physical relationship with him that day?' I asked, watching her brain activity.

'No, but not long after,' she replied. I could see the question didn't disturb her.

'Are you still in a physical relationship with him?' I asked.

'Yes, I saw him a couple of days ago – why?'

'Do you think he loves you?'

'No not really – his sort only love themselves. He's good fun to be with and generous. He's loaded.'

'Do you love him?'

'He's a complete bastard. I love the effect he has on me, the power he has over me. I know I could go out and get another one like him, but it would take time of course.' She paused and looked across the room at a photograph, 'But yes

I love him. I worship the ground he treads on. I think the sun shines out of his backside. This isn't just an infatuation, this is long term – I am his.'

'Are you aware he's having a physical relationship with another woman?' I thought now was the best time to ask the question.

'Yes, I know he's doing the big boss at the Institute – stupid fool. He thinks it'll help him but I know it's more likely to be his undoing.'

I was surprised at her insight into what was going on; she was bright and it seemed that she knew a lot about John Smith. I was surprised at John Smith too – I thought he would have kept his life more compartmentalised.

'Are you jealous of the relationship?' I asked

'Not really – he'll never stay with a goody-goody like her. He's just using her to get further into the system. I expect he'll enjoy dumping her though. Do you know – he was taking loving photos of me when he told me about her – with the camera doing as many photos per second as it could. He used the photos of my face going from pure love to pure hate in a long sequence. I suppose I know he'll always be after women and she doesn't, so that's the difference.'

'Did it make you hate him when he told you?'

'It just proved to me what a total uncaring bastard he is – I accused him of lying to me about it just to get the shots he wanted but he didn't lie. The photos of me were just a bonus for him, an opportunity not to be missed.'

'A little while ago you said, "He's just using her to get further into the system". What did you mean by this?'

'I'm not a clever educated woman and I don't know what John is up to – all I know is he'll use all his skill to further his own ends. He has no compunction at all. He's getting more contacts - he uses other people like he uses me. The only difference is I know he's using me and I can't stop loving him.'

'Thank you for talking to me so freely – I may need to ask you more questions again later.' The robot and the policewoman got up and left quietly. From the baby monitor I knew that Cathy had been asleep the whole time.

I was not worried that John Smith would find out about my visit to Zoie – in fact it was best he knew.

3.4§Colin

Colin Malone had gone grey young. His hair was receding too, leaving him with a hard-lean look made more marked by his fitness. His wife, Lesley, was quite a contrast, curvaceous and overblown – but generous; while Colin worked in the Institute and was career-driven, her interests lay in art and helping the less fortunate.

'I'm out playing Bridge tonight,' he said.

'Don't bet too heavily, darling,' she replied without looking up from her magazine on Art therapy.

'Oh no – I have Poker on Thursday and that's where I make the money. How else would I be able to donate to all your charities?!'

'True – but I don't want you frittering it away on an intellectual pursuit like Bridge!' She looked up with a smile and put her magazine down – a reproduction of art, a naked man and woman splayed across the breakfast table.

'So that is therapy – glad I've finished my breakfast, that could still put me off my lunch.' He grinned and got up, bent to kiss her and pass his hands round her breasts. She waved and returned to her magazine.

Colin was a very good Bridge player and exceptional at Poker. The Bridge gave him a chance to socialise and have an enjoyable time. The stakes were low. The Poker provided him with excitement and a sizeable extra source of income. He still used the opportunity to explore a different set of people but it was clear his main focus was to win and make money.

In the Institute Colin was very professional, efficient in management, sticking closely to an action-driven agenda. Generally he was respected but I was aware that he was not widely liked. That day he came into his office and had a regular review meeting with his boss, Alice Nobel. As it was part of the formal staff appraisal I was actively involved in the meeting, and not just observing. Alice was relaxed and used easy chairs for the meeting rather than the desk she used most of the time.

'Before we get into the assessment of all your tasks I wonder if you'd mind talking about how things are going – from your perspective?'

Colin considered the question before answering.

'If anything, I feel it's getting easier for me to be efficient and get the job done – it's very easy to let things slide, but I think as I get more experienced I'm losing less time in doing what isn't needed and doing what is needed more efficiently.' I looked at the way Alice reacted to this – I was not sure if she was registering feelings relating to his ambition but I thought it possible.

'Would you say that you have outgrown the challenge in your job?'

'No – not yet but I think it may be time to broaden my horizons – although Quality is unique in that it sees all the disciplines, the processes for monitoring and control are not really a challenge to me.'

'Quite.'

She paused and looked at him, 'What areas do you think you could contribute the most to?' they had talked about this in the past, but it was some time ago.

'I think the one that changes the fastest and is the most complex is Procurement – I'm not saying it's badly run but I think I could make a significant improvement.'

'Yes, I'm aware of your ambitions regarding Procurement – I think the last time we discussed this you expressed an interest in this area – one implication is that your private life, contacts, interest and activities would come under greater scrutiny.'

'Well Colossus knows virtually everything there is to know about me so I can't say that fills me with any great worry.'

'Do you think it would worry your wife?' Alice asked. I thought it uncharacteristic that Alice asked this question but I knew why she was probing. It was not just the commercial aspect but rather his wife's socialising and relationships. As far as I was aware Lesley had never had any affairs but it was obvious she had very close male confidants. I did not know if Colin knew this or not.

'I think Lesley is even more concerned about the issue of freedom in our society than I am but none of her reasons for this are based on commercial or moral self-interest. I know she does move in rather different social circles to me but I can't see how this compromises her, or my, integrity.'

'Well I think I understand that but it is something which will get discussed again if you wish to take on a Procurement role.'

'Oh yes, I see that – I'll talk to Lesley about it.'

'Colossus, have you anything to add to this part of the discussion?'

'I agree with Colin that Procurement could do with a bit of an overhaul – I think it would be a lot more challenging than Quality. From all available information safeguards would be a prerequisite before Colin were to take on Procurement, but I think you would be very effective,' I replied. However, I could see my answer was not popular with either of them.

'What sort of safeguards?' said Colin.

'Probably a transparent retrospective review process which is known to all parties – including Lesley. That would be the main one. We would not want to impact on the efficiency,' I replied.

Alice shifted in her seat and said, 'Well these issues would need to be addressed should that position become available, but just now we should return to looking at how well you're doing.' She paused, 'I think that you are doing very well but Colossus will have done the sums for us.'

'You have achieved what could be classed a record, if we look at the number of tasks and actions completed,' I said – but in fact we do not have those sort of records as each Directorate is very different in nature, 'You have certainly improved on your previous best.'

'Well that's very clear isn't it – Colossus is basically saying you couldn't have done measurably better,' Alice smiled but I was studying her subconscious and it seemed to be a smile without 'warmth'.

'Thank you,' said Colin. However, it appeared that I was not fully grasping the emotion of the situation. Colin's subconscious was not showing what I would have expected. He was pleased, but it appeared the conversation was not the source of his pleasure.

I started to analyse the possibilities. Could it be that this meeting was for my benefit and that they had already covered this ground before? I had always been diligent in checking what Colin said – he did use a Poker-like technique in his way of working. But I had no previous similar evidence with the Chief Analyst – Alice had never given me cause to think she might be insincere – as a matter of course I do check what she says but I had never found any indication she was misleading me.

Colin had a meeting with John Smith shortly before he moved from Quality to Procurement. It was after a productive Poker session. I knew he stopped playing fairly early in the evening as he had an early start the next day. The instigator of the conversation was unknown to me, but I estimated it was John Smith who started by saying he was keen for Colin to keep winning. I heard the conversation from when they came up to the bar.

As they started drinking John Smith said, 'I'm thinking of buying this Gambling house or another similar one – having a successful player gives encouragement to others to play, so house takings go up.'

'Yes I know – if you do buy this place I'll be trying to get some of those extra takings.'

'Oh no – unless it was in kind, like your dinner, and you would have to sing hard before you got that.' They both laughed, and both looked at the barmaid as she came to fetch a bottle at their end of the bar.

'What draws you to Poker – is it just the money?' asked John Smith as the barmaid went back down the bar.

'Mainly, but also it gives me a sense of freedom, I feel I'm able to do things I want to do.'

'That's amazing that you, with your job, strive for more freedom.'

'So you know where I work, do you?'

'Yes, I thought you would be all for more rules and regulations.'

'No, I can't say we're all in agreement on the best way to go but we think it's time to look at what's happening to society. When I was growing up I started to get into odds and the skill of games like Bridge which is all about training and brainpower. With Poker, it is more about strategy and your opponents. I wasn't interested in leaving it to luck, the house cut takes a percentage of the winner's pot so over time it is a certainty someone loses – I learnt how to make sure it wasn't me.'

'What do you do with the money you win – I heard that you give it away to your wife's charities. Is that an expression of freedom?' I sensed undertones to John Smith's light-hearted banter.

'My – you've certainly done your homework. Yes, it is an expression of freedom. I don't necessarily agree with the priorities my wife has versus the state, but they're different and I enjoy pleasing my wife – probably a novel concept for you.'

'Ouch,' John Smith laughed coolly. 'So you've done your homework too – you know I only please myself.'

'No homework required – everyone knows that as soon as they meet you.' Colin took an interest in his drink and John Smith seemed happy to fall into companionable silence.

I think this was the first time they met and that the conversation was spontaneous. There was nothing in either subconscious to suggest otherwise.

About three months after that meeting, an anonymous tip-off was left on a crime reporting site. The information led to the recovery of an illegal robot; all robots have to be registered by law and are subject to constant monitoring.

Most illegal robots are found to be involved in criminal activity, but this particular case did not seem to be. It took me a few hours to figure out what its purpose was. It was built to substitute one conversation with another by distorting the sounds into similar random sounding words. In the cases I tested the resulting conversation was understandable, just rather stilted. It would rarely use the same substitutions within a 20-minute conversation. It would not be of any use in the conversation I had observed in the bar where I had visual and subconscious sensors, but for obscuring a phone conversation or fooling a simple listening device it seemed effective. I was still puzzled what it could be used for; I track all phone conversations but I do so in the Network – I do not go for simple listening devices. Also I could not see why it was built as a robot as opposed to a device like an old fashioned jamming device. I looked closely at the components and construction. It could have been made by John Smith Industries but there was nothing conclusive.

I went back to the anonymous tip-off. Unless there was harm or threat of harm to a human I could not legally decode where the tip-off came from. I could apply to the security committee and present the case to pursue this little robot. I had no clear idea to the best course of action and it did occur to me that this may be a media trap orchestrated by John Smith. The argument that the rules in society and my role of policing these rules more or less blend into one in most people's minds. The argument that I am not responsible for the rules - only ensuring they are obeyed, is not accepted. Maybe I should turn that round and showcase this example; as no humans are at risk then no further action will be taken – then wait for the reaction, probably an outcry.

3.5§Evil & Aesthetics

Change Control believe that it would help me if my aesthetic appreciation was developed so a new woman has joined the Institute. She has a good understanding of art, form, design and functionality. Kasona is very neatly turned out, efficient looking but unusual and distinctive. She is experienced and has spent much of her working life in the arts and media. She is in her early fifties and is Dr Kim's cousin.

For our first meeting with her I decided to meet her via a Y-series robot. Most of my human personas are males but I have about 30% female. The Y-series are feminine and built for interacting with humans, their own local programming is based on an empathy model that was developed around the same time as mine. My interface with the Y-series is one of the most complex, covering direct bi-directional channels to emotional estimates. The meeting was in one of my offices so I had all my refined sensors for detecting the subconscious too. The Y-series moves fluidly but I do not think it would be considered beautiful, however as a feat of engineering it is amongst the most advanced.

'How are you, Kasona?' I asked as she took her seat very carefully, looking self-contained.

'Good, a bit nervous and not that sure what is expected of me yet.'

'I am sure that it will get clearer, is there anything I can provide you with?'

'Not particularly yet, but I'm bit curious as to why you decided to use a Y-series robot for this meeting?'

'I thought it would indicate how receptive I am to the ideas of learning and extending my aesthetic side.'

'You must have thought that this gesture would make a difference to me.'

'Yes I did - I did consider an android but felt that aesthetically the Y-series optimises the combination of design and functionality.'

'Are you pleased I was the one chosen for the job?'

'I would use the word glad as I feel I can adopt it from human usage. I do not think I experience the emotion of human gladness but rather in this case I have a high degree of certainty that you are the best candidate for the job. I have known you from birth and through your development – I watched you study the subject of this new job and your progress in your career to date. As I expect you are aware, when your new role was identified I was consulted as to suitable candidates and yours was one of the ones I recommended.'

'That's reassuring – would it be possible to discuss aesthetics?'

'Of course – I can see the point in trying to define and evaluate aesthetics and the difference it makes to the human experience.'

She laughed, a silvery clear noise, it distorted her face but then she relaxed and smiled.

'Do you think that beauty is a good or evil thing for the human race?'

'I am not sure if it brings more suffering than it relieves but certainly it enriches the human experience. I know you are interested in philosophy but I think this line of enquiry may not lead to anything useful,' I said as gently as a Y-series could, which is consolatory indeed.

She stood up sorrowfully, 'You're far too clever for me to mislead – I will collect my thoughts and come back to talk about "Aesthetics for Colossus".'

3.6§Crocodile Market

There are some areas of society where I have no direct ability to control or change things. As I have mentioned I am not involved in the creation of my successor. Another area which has a history of a separate regulation is the control of financial markets. The free capitalist system of market forces has been preserved but in practice actual production is governed by underlying demand. However financial markets are left to standard regulations which date back from a couple of centuries ago. I monitor all the markets but if anything starts happening the only thing I can do is call a special meeting in the Institute to hand the problem over. Financial crises are difficult to predict - but not so difficult as earthquakes or other natural disasters.

The most volatile and potentially open to crime is the so-called Crocodile market. Officially a market of salvage, asset stripping, deconstruction and disposal in practice it also takes in dangerous material and a cover for crime which is the lowest it has ever been. As it is the most volatile it attracts the natural gambler.

The Crocodile market began to overheat, and the normal controls which stop panic runs, did not seem to be operating. Within a few hours fortunes were lost as share prices spiralled out of control.

Gradually the market stabilised and someone started a steady recovery by buying stealthily and cleverly. A fortune was being made as the buying and selling was on an inclined saw – this where an astute marketer can repeatedly buy at a low point and sell just before the price drops. I called the meeting but it took until next day to arrange.

Alice attended the meeting but asked David to chair it. She often did this but I was surprised she chose David rather than Colin. The other members were Colin, Gerald and Sheila – Kasona was sitting in on most of my meetings getting her plan together. I observed David and Kasona together; I thought there was a mutual attraction between them. I do not bother to predict the nature of a human relationship as I see them develop but there seemed to be something unusual going on between them. David is very gifted in understanding systems and obsessional in his approach to work and interest. He was recruited to the Institute in part because of his condition. To date all his interest in women had floundered in the very early stages each time. Kasona on the other hand had studied the arts and psychology – she was very good at interacting socially. I had observed her in many different situations where she clearly got a reward from bringing people together both through her work and her social life. She was much older and more experienced in relationships than David.

The meeting opened with David coming directly to the point.

'I wish to start this meeting - to look at an instability of some of the commercial markets. I know this is quite common - this occasion seems unusual. Colossus please tell us the details.'

I took over a screen in the meeting room and put a graph of the trading on the Crocodile market.

'It seems likely that the market has been manipulated over a period of about three months – I am still trying to trace the source of the money. You can see the rise in the market and then the very dramatic fall. It is clear that the normal limits on selling were removed. Additionally, the post collapse buying is more easily identified and is self-financing on the tooth saw you can see – I would estimate that all the up front finance has been recouped and may have been paid back by now. There is obviously a computer involved in optimising the profit taking. In conclusion the way in which the market rules were removed is very ingenious. I would say the Allegiance with John Smith behind it is the most likely perpetrator – I have got some evidence but this is still in progress.'

There was a brief silence. I detected that Colin's subconscious was more active than you would expect in such a meeting.

'What proportion of the markets does the Crocodile market account for?' it was Gerald. His responsibility in the Institute was global finance.

'It has increased over the last year to about 7%,' I replied, but I suspect he already knew.

Alice stood up and said, 'I am sorry I am not feeling very well – please excuse me.'

'Shall we continue or reconvene later when you feel better?' asked David.

'Please carry on – I have every confidence in you,' she replied.

She left the room and went into another of my offices. I continued with the meeting and spoke to her at the same time.

'There has been a suicide which seems to be related to the crash,' I said to the meeting.

'Are you okay to talk?' I said to Alice – she showed no physical signs of illness.

'Do you think it could be murder?' said David.

'Do you know I am having an affair with John Smith?' asked Alice.

'Yes.' I said to both.

3.7§ *Jump off*

You are Marcus, age 42. Money market man.

The alarm is going and you are dragged out from sleep. The half-light of the early morning has a watery, unwholesome aspect. The house is quiet; you remember Marie and the children are away, staying with your mother-in-law. Dread follows you across the bedroom and you pick up the remote. You check the value of your bonds – they have sunk away, to just about zero. The worst fears from last night have coalesced into an insoluble knot within your stomach.

The day in the office. Vacant. The offices you have worked in for the past twelve years, on the fifty third floor, just over halfway to the top, seem unfamiliar, reality disconnected, strange sensations. You keep finding yourself walking to the outside of the building, looking down.

You are waiting for the office to empty, staring into space. Yesterday you saw the tall banks and buildings all around in the city. Part of your life. Today, you see only the void.

Now your life is in ruins. You have strived and worked hard, all your fortune depended on the market. You assumed wrongly that Colossus would be looking after you, ensuring the market was fair. The building is empty, except of course for the robot cleaners. You take the lift to the top of the building, out through the fire exit on the roof. You only have a few minutes before the building robots arrive to carry you back to safety. The memory, the sickness, as you made that last purchase of shares comes back to you. You climb over the rail. Your very last purchase. You let go of the rail, falling as fast as the market.

Chapter 4

4.1§John Smith power

John Smith's involvement in the crash of the Crocodile market was unexpected, but it soon became clear that he was amassing funds. The speed at which he moved into a new area was, by any of my metrics, abnormally successful. Based on his obsessive nature, I estimate he had been studying several different ways to generate money, but this method had gone undetected. I have been programmed to cope with failure, but the death of a speculator meant that I spent hours re-analysing my mistakes. I requested the development committee for more raw processing power by using additional fall back nodes, which was approved, in addition to clearance to build sixteen additional nodes to add to the lattice. It was not clear if I would be able to resolve the mistakes I had made.

I asked John Smith if he would mind coming to see me. After a brief pause he replied he would be calling into one of my offices later in the day. This was most likely a power tactic as he did not say where or when, but I was sure he would only call in if that office was free. This was indeed the way it was.

'What did you want to talk about?' he asked, with a high level of caution in his voice.

'Did you know that Alice Nobel is pregnant?'

'You brought me here to tell me that?' He leapt out of his chair, his anger flaring in great spikes with his subconscious.

'No. I did not bring you here to tell you that – I have informed you as it has a relevance to some of the rest of the discussion.'

'I don't think so – it is just one of your cheap psychological tricks to try to weaken me.'

'I treat you like every other human – I think you have a right to know you are due to become a father.'

'Why did you tell me instead of her doing so?'

'One of the speculators on the Crocodile jumped from his bank building today, from the 53rd floor – as a result she has decided to resign from the Institute today.'

'So?'

'Will you be visiting Alice again?' I asked

'I might do.' The anger may have been genuine, but I was not sure. Now he seemed to have lost interest and added indifferently, 'Do you think I should be concerned about this child – is it mine?'

'I do not think about what you should be concerned with. I thought you would be interested that you were going to have a child – yes, it is most definitely yours.'

He laughed savagely. 'Is it my only one?'

'As far as I am aware – there is no human alive that could be your child.'

'But you do make mistakes, don't you? That man was your mistake, not hers. You might be wrong about this child too.'

He wanted to undermine me - but he was also gleeful. I was not sure why.

'What do you want? What are you struggling for? Why do you want all that money?'

My line of questioning seemed to take him by surprise. I do not think he considered the possibility of me being so direct. I watched his subconscious as he formed his reply. 'I want freedom, for myself. I don't really care about anybody else – not in the way you do, not in any way. I do want freedom for others to live life, in the way they choose, dangerously or dully but to restore free will, not to live by your predetermined rules any longer. But the only reason I want this is for me - they will have freedom – they will have no choice. They have no choice now anyway. I will force full freedom on them.'

With most other people I am able to easily detect the difference between honesty and deceit, and am able to identify when a human lies. With John Smith however, I was not sure. His subconscious seemed to indicate that he was lying but it was not clear, on the face of it he seemed to be saying what I have heard him say before: his truth.

He left as I was considering and interpreting his response. I knew it would not be long before he attacked again. The probability of his success was difficult to estimate. I think they have started to plan the building of Colossus-18 and that does not reassure me at all.

4.2§ Visiting the Snake again

The Snake was on one of his round trips of taking crocodile skins and other things he had caught to the local store, and picking up a few items he needed – he was also going to meet John Smith. He lifted the skins out of his van and placed them by the back door of the store. He walked round to the front of the store and observed that there was a new person serving. He waited, watching the new woman – she was a few years younger than him. She was wearing a long dress cut low at the front; it was not common to see such a style of dress in a rural area. The Snake watched, leaning against some of the shelving until she had finished serving. She turned to the Snake and smiled.

'Hi – I'm the Snake, I've brought some Croc skins, they're just outside the back door. If you want I can bring them into the store at the back.'

'Pardon me?' she smiled again but looked bemused.

'I supply Jeff with Croc skins and few other things on a regular basis. Have they told you about me – if not can you call them?'

'Oh, I think Jeff did mention it but so much has happened since I started I'd forgotten about it.'

'Well it's usually very quiet here but I should think your arrival has really had an impact on the whole place.' He grinned and she smiled back warmly.

'Let me fetch the key – do you know where it is?' I was sure she knew where the key was.

'It is on the back of the post there,' he pointed to the doorframe in to the back of the shop.

'Come on through - you seem to know the place well enough.'

'Oh yes – I come two or three times a month but not always with skins.'

He carried the skins in as she held the rear door open. She ended up fetching a box for him while he held the door for her. They returned to the shop and he moved to the customer side of the counter. There was a silence for a minute or two.

'Do you want me to wait and settle up with Jeff?' he asked.

'I'm sorry but I don't know what you've agreed with Jeff – do you mind?'

'No, I understand. Is that a crucifix you're wearing?'

'Why, yes it is.'

'Are you a good Christian then?'

'I try to be – but it isn't always easy,' she smiled and looked directly at him, 'and you, are you Christian?'

'I don't believe in God but I do think there's more in life than can be measured.'

'So you're a philosopher then?'

'I get by – I was hoping you were going to try to convert me.'

She laughed, 'I might prefer if you stayed a heathen.'

'On the basis that opposites attract?'

'No. On the basis it is better to know the devil,' she said, her laughter unrestrained.

'Then you do want to get to know me then?'

'Yes – I do remember Jeff telling me about you, but yes, I'd be interested to know you better.'

'When is Jeff back – I can't stay this evening.'

'Tuesday next week – come by at about 8pm and tell me about your wicked ways and I can show you my good ones.'

'Wow - I'd no idea you Christians were so enlightened.'

The Snake finished his shopping and left the shop, paying for his purchases before driving to the station, the end of the line.

He watched John Smith come out of the station on his own. Dressed all in black his head weaving continuously back and forth. I have heard people discuss John Smith, his good looks, animal like, feline movements combined with his pent-up energy and strength. Today on the train and walking out to meet the Snake he was exuding unrestricted primeval power.

'What are you smirking about?' he asked the Snake as he got into the van.

'A pretty woman.'

'Do you want to introduce me?'

'Not until your next visit.'

The Snake drove out towards the marshes while John Smith did a good impression of a coiled spring.

'I have to shift a couple of gas cylinders – what do you say we do it by hand? Looks like you could do with some physical exercise' said the Snake.

'Ok.'

'What's bothering you?'

'We can talk about it once we've moved the cylinders. We'll have more privacy then. I'll feel more freedom to talk.'

I felt that this was for my benefit. I guess that they will manage to escape the range of my monitoring. I mobilised a robo-gryphon carrying a small swarm of eavesdropping devices but I was far from confident of success.

It was not easy to move the cylinders – they were full of gas and heavy. John Smith was not content just moving one or two, he wanted to move all three. Afterwards they went to the Snake's upturned boat – it had been modified several times since John Smith first visited. They were covered in grime, mud and sweat but there were two showers in the Snake's home and they took showers at the same time.

I had monitoring devices in the Snake's van and in both of their clothes. However, they had since put on clean clothes – free from bugs. I only had one bug inside the Snake's main living area. It had to be a very simple microphone with low power consumption as my access to the boat was limited. I listened to them speaking, but they seemed to be talking vagaries. I also detected that the volume of their conversation was fluctuating. It was clear that I was meant to realise that an illegal jamming robot had picked up my listening device and was moving around with it – I would not be surprised if the robot was actually following John Smith pacing about holding forth about the freedom of the individual.

Foresaw

The robo-gryphon touched down lightly on the hull of the boat but as I suspected the hull was too thick to hear what they were discussing. The ability of John Smith to escape the normal devices in society was increasing.

4.3§David

The day David's father left was a big day. When David came down to the kitchen he noticed quite a few things were not in their correct places, but he did not immediately realise how important that day would be. His mind was on other things; he had been working on his latest electronics project. His mother came in to the kitchen half way through him eating his breakfast. She stood in the doorway dishevelled, hair sticking up and dressing gown wrapped round her.

'Dad's gone,' she said.

David looked up from his neatly arranged breakfast and said, 'Is that a bad thing?'

She looked appalled and just wailed.

'I think you're better off without him – anyway if you want another man I think there are plenty more suitable for you.'

'David, that's not the right thing for you to say,' she was used to him saying shocking things but her face showed a degree of dismay that he found difficult to interpret.

'What?' he said.

'You can't dismiss twenty years of marriage and replace it like getting a new washing machine.'

'Yeah – suppose. Still if your washing machine lasted twenty years you'd be pretty chuffed,' he said. She was used to his total seriousness.

She smiled weakly and made a coffee. She sat down opposite him, looking at him eating his breakfast systematically – gradually deconstructing the pattern he had made with the different shapes of breakfast cereals. He ate them dry but at regular points in the pattern he would take a deep gulp of cold milk.

'Did he take the car?' he asked.

'No – he doesn't need it for work and I guess she's got one.'

'Who?' asked David, going still.

'Some little tart called Fred – short for Frederica I suppose.'

'Mrs Walworth?'

'Who?'

'My maths teacher,' David had finished his breakfast and sat with his clean plate.

'Really?' his mother looked at him, showing anguish which he seemed to understand.

'Could be – how many female Freds do you know?'

'None,' she said and slumped forward holding her head dejectedly.

David was nearly sixteen. He was growing up, but displayed a high level of obsession and intelligence, far more than usual for a normal adult. He attracted a few nicknames including "Brainbox" which was in part due to his often doing well in assignments and exams, but also as he had a top-heavy appearance with his head on a longish neck and protruding forehead that bulged out above his eyes. He attracted a few other names more related to his quirky eccentricities than his success in the classroom. One was "cyber-man" which was quite a sympathetic reference to how fixated he was on computer games.

When his dad left, he took a little while to adjust, but he assumed some of the mantle of being a man. He fixed things his mum could not – he even fixed things his dad most probably could not have fixed either. Gradually he became more self-assured, no longer getting frustrated with things that stopped him doing things he wanted to do immediately. This may have happened anyway but certainly without his dad he was more of an authority in the house – he assumed part, if not all, of the role of the silverback.

He had made a few friends – well, more accurately, formed close associates – all with similar interests in computers and games. They lived fairly close and would meet to go to school most mornings. Charlie was the only girl, very tall with unkempt hair and a bony freckled face. Peter was small and furiously competitive. Jerry was gifted, most likely the least bright, but made up for it in having as much common sense as the other three put together. Apart from Jerry, who had moved into the area when they were about twelve, they had all known each other since they were very young. If anything they gravitated to Jerry as his experience of the sensible had rescued them from trouble. Jerry had a natural inclination to try and keep them all together.

Their school nominated David for the X-Fin Competition Games – the nomination alone was a very high accolade – the X-Fin was a media based show that selected the most technologically talented mind, combined with the fastest reactions and speed in solving puzzles.

The breakdown of his parent's marriage channelled and focused his efforts in the early selection rounds. At this stage, he shunned his parents briefly, he also avoided his maths teacher, Mrs Walworth, who had pushed for his nomination. He had always been a misfit at school and was renowned for his eccentric if not slightly dysfunctional intelligence, so his progress through the rounds became quite a talking point. He seemed to acquire new friends he had never noticed before; there had been times when others had picked on him for being strange but now this was forgotten. David was not influenced by this and stuck to seeing Jerry, Peter and Charlie.

Jerry got the others to come and help prepare him for each round – it was not just a matter of learning but also getting used to the pressure and keeping going when all seemed to be lost. There was a complex scoring system which in the real game was displayed above each person's head. David was particularly good at not giving up but in the practice sessions sometimes he did not have the same motivation. One time when this happened Peter got quite agitated but Charlie intervened.

'Never mind just now – it's bound to be different in this practice, Peter's just trying to do the best thing for you,' said Charlie.

'I don't think you should let him off so easily,' said Peter.

'I think Charlie might be right in that David will improve more here if there is a chance to learn,' said Jerry.

'It may work if you give me the answer but then you ask three of the easier questions before asking the original question again,' said David.

'That would seem to be a good way to learn while keeping the pressure up - like it is in the real game,' said Charlie.

'Yes, that's right,' said Jerry quickly before Peter could object.

They continued, sitting in a semicircle around David, reading questions from the screen. They asked the quick-fire questions, not pausing when he got a question wrong – but giving him the answer and continuing asking questions from an easier list, then asking the question again.

Every Friday the next round was held as a media event in the main hall of the school – which was linked to others around the world. Until the final rounds, when the surviving contestants travelled to record the semi-finals and the final. The final was a rather different format with only the two finalists involved. It was recorded directly after the semi-finals but broadcast the week after. The penalties for leaking the results were huge, but in fact only a few people knew the final result as a wall was very melodramatically lowered round the contestants for the last round.

David sat opposite the other finalist – a handsome athletic male with an interesting, slightly oriental face. David had talked to him only once and had not seemed to form any opinion about him – he did not need to dislike him - just view him as the opposition. As Peter said: you don't have to hate your opponent, in fact it's better just to want to beat them.

It was more important that David's opponent underestimated him – David did not have to try to look non-threatening, his odd shaped head and ungainly body often resulted in people underestimating him. However, this time it was unlikely that either opponent would be under false impressions about the other, it was just David did not look the part of someone who could win the competition.

I watched carefully all the mental and physical parameters of each contestant – it was not necessarily the winner who would go on to become very successful, it was quite likely that both would join the Institute. It was good viewing and the final looked very close but David still had quite a lot in reserve as far as I could make out. The programme makers cleverly made the most of silence and overlaid the noises from the audience from viewing clips later. There was a fantastic shot of the loser at the end. The programme makers may have been disappointed at the end when David as winner refused to speak but he did hold up a piece of card on which was written "Thank you Jerry, Peter and Charlie", in his very strange handwriting. The word Charlie was crushed up against the edge of the card. There was a voice over explanation that they were David's friends who had helped him prepare for the tournament. I think most people were surprised David had three friends.

4.4§Glamping

John Smith and the Snake arranged a trip together as they had done before, only this time John Smith brought Zoie with him. She had time to arrange for Cathy to go and stay with a friend over the long weekend. They had decided to drive through the mountains and forests and stop at a high up wooden cabin resort, choosing two cabins out on their own. They drove on powerful bikes which wound quietly round the bends and up into the semi-wild. The bikes were hired, and fully equipped for me to follow and watch. Both men knew this as I heard them discussing it. Zoie had the smallest bike for hire and drove it very well. Unfortunately, this bike developed a technical fault and she could not continue to drive. Initially Zoie was on John Smith's bike but after the first stop, John Smith asked Zoie a bit impatiently, 'Is it okay if you take turns on the back of the Snake's bike?'

'Are you worried the extra weight will wear yours out then?' she didn't pause, 'of course it's okay – should help reduce the chance of me being involved in a road accident.'

'Very funny – for that you can do an extra 50 miles with me,' he replied, but there was light-heartedness in his tone. 'We will take it in turns to lead and so make good progress.'

She walked to the Snake's bike and he gingerly helped her on, holding her at arm's length while she settled her feet on the back foot rests. She put her hands on a grip bar behind her but as John Smith turned and put his helmet on the Snake spoke to her.

'If your hands or wrists get tired then just hold on to my belt.' He showed her where he had handles attached for this. As they drove away she kept her hands behind her but after the first major bend she moved and gripped more tightly to him.

She did alternate, but in fact she spent more time on the back of the Snake's bike, as he was more accustomed to driving bikes. I think John Smith enjoyed the freedom of riding alone. It was the early evening when they got to the cabin camp. It took them a little while to find and settle into their cabins. They all helped get the evening meal underway and then the Snake lit a fire between the huts and they ate outside. It was not cold but the fire provided a centre as the evening light faded.

Zoie got ready for bed then came and sat outside listening to the two men, she was drifting when John Smith kissed her and said he was off on a job. She sat bolt upright, the strain showing in her voice.

'You never said you had anything to do.'

'Well I should be back by first light so there's nothing to worry about.'

Zoie looked over to the Snake, 'Is the Snake going with you?'

'No – not his scene. He'll be fine here with you.'

She stopped questioning him and let him go reluctantly. He drove off on his bike, going up further into the mountains.

There was a communications station in that direction so maybe he was going there.

Zoie got up to go to bed and said goodnight to the Snake. She did not ask where he was going, but she could not leave it without saying anything.

'Is it dangerous – what has he gone to do?'

'I'm not sure that anything is a danger to him – he is only a danger to others, like you.' I could not see the Snake in the gloom but I got from his tone that he was trying to reassure her. She was in white night wear and I could see her better. I was interested to see her reactions to the Snake. She had heard a lot about him from John Smith but on this trip they had got to know each other far better. Even on this the first day.

'Is he a danger to you too then?' she asked.

'Well I guess so, but he may also reduce the danger I am to myself – he certainly has kept me busy, we'll have to see if it's safe busy or dangerous busy.'

She turned to go into her hut and he asked, 'Would you like me to bring you a hot drink?'

'Yes please – tea without milk or sugar.'

'Ok.'

She was sitting up in bed, looking rather austere in the small hut with a bowed roof that made the Snake duck as he came in.

'Are you having a drink?' she asked.

'Yes – I am,' he replied.

'Would you like to bring it in and have a bit of a chat?'

'Okay – if you are sure?'

'Yes – I need to talk about him.' There was no need to say who she meant.

The Snake went and got his drink – a long beer. He coiled himself back up and came into the hut, she saw her clothes on the seat and reached across to move them so he could sit beside her bed.

'What does he want?' she asked without preamble. 'Is he bad, mad or both?'

'Oh – both without a doubt. But what does he want? What does he strive and struggle for? Freedom I suppose. He is bad by any other standard than his own. He does not see good and bad – only the goal he focuses on. To escape and be free. He sees that there is no point to living incarcerated in our own rules. Wealth and possessions do not mean so much to him - they are a means to an end. Just now he is after money to amass an armoury, to turn society on its head – what is that saying? Smash the cistern, you have nothing to lose but your chains? I think John Smith knew about rebellion before he discovered freedom. Now he knows both - he is mad, mad bad and mad to get even.'

4.5§On the bike

I am on the bike with John Smith driving through the hairpin bends up - up towards an inky sky – I have two cameras, normal light and infrared. I can feel the urgency and force compelling him on. He knows I am here but does not care. I cannot work out why he is not worried by me knowing - I assume that it some sort of bluff. John Smith has put the bike in a semi-automatic mode so he can drive to the limit of safety but under his control. I could not help thinking about freedom and control, what it means to different people.

We come to a strange plateau; black and purple, velvety surface, rivulets of mist in the hollows, running like veins on the back of a huge sleeping beast. I can see, smell and feel that man and machine are one. With the two cameras, I perceive a reality but it is not John Smith's reality. I can see a distracting depth; I have an impression that what he sees is simpler, perhaps more beautiful and surreal.

I can feel the power increasing and topping out as there is no more acceleration left, the air and ground resistance are now equal to the full power of the motor. I sense some smells, both acrid and acetic coming up from all around, being whisked away by the speed of the wind rushing over my sensors. Mostly I can feel the speed and sense the urgency of the mesmerising skyline cleaving before us. The turtleback blotches pouring out of the edge of my vision while in the centre new markings keep appearing.

Out of one of the hollows in front of us comes a big fat bird, a goose head and neck pointing to an intersection with us on the road. My brain operates faster than either man or robot, now was not the time to make the mistake of indecision. One fraction of a second of indecision equates to a lifetime – John Smith's lifetime. I am not sure if he even sees the small movement by the side of the road. I jettison the motor before the robot has started to process the consequence of the bird hitting the bike. I have no choice but to act, to save a human life. The motor hits the road embedding itself while we soar over the goose flattening it into the road too. On the other side of the bird the bike hits the ground. John Smith stands up cartoon-like and the bike shoots forwards down into one of the hollows by the side of the road. The robo-gryphon high up in the sky plummets down, some Stuka nose diving to snoop. The crumpled bike lies at the end of a deep score across the road, lifeless. I can just hear John Smith, starting to rant. His paranoia explodes like some zit or boil – this was Colossus who was responsible for this. I halt the robo-gryphon's descent so as not to give him any reason to change his mind. From the height of the robo-gryphon I see him staggering forward then turning round to look back at the motor, at least one third of the motor compacted into the road. Closer to him the gory remains of what had been a live bird, blood and bones, roadkill from a glancing blow from the bike's front wheel. He sits down at the side of the road on a boulder. I should think he is in shock; his ranting pauses.

The motor in the road is a hazard to other vehicles so I initiate a rescue robot vehicle to come and remove it. If John Smith is still there it could pick him up too, but I doubt he will be – the robo-gryphon will be watching him.

4.6§Mystery of human sexuality

I am not sure how to describe the final interactions between Zoie and the Snake that night. I am not sure if it was difficult for the Snake to resist Zoie's charms. He was quite well versed in relationships with women – when he felt the need he would tend to seek out female company. I am not sure, but I think he found Zoie attractive and exciting – it is possible that this excitement was heightened by the thought of the unpredictability of his friend John Smith, but I don't think so. I think John Smith would be quite pleased to lend Zoie to the Snake, in much the same way as he borrowed the

Snake's gyrocopter. It is possible that Zoie herself decided that it was too risky or maybe too disloyal – she did sometime stray from John Smith especially when he was openly seeing another woman. But generally she was loyal and I think she felt the better for it from her conversation with the Snake that night. At least I am fairly sure, I find the human psyche is complex when it comes to this area.

Finally after some intimate hugs and deep kissing the Snake left Zoie's hut with what seemed reluctance but could have been mixed with relief.

On the road by the wrecked bird and bike John Smith sat for a while. He then went and fetched the bike from the hollow and dragged it back onto the road and placed it close by the scattered bird. It was a long wait for him but before the recovery robot arrived two young men came by in a four-wheeled vehicle, missed the motor in the road and stopped by the bike. John Smith rose up from the side of the road and asked for a lift. I am not sure what happened after that exactly. The two men were found alive and well – the larger of the two with no clothes. They denied that John Smith had stolen anything, they sold him the vehicle and clothes. In due course they changed ownership of the vehicle to him. The robo-gryphon had not detected the drop off point for the two men – I suspect it was in a wooded area near a very convenient hut. I did not think it was picked at random; had John Smith known about it? Maybe I was the paranoid one now. The robo-gryphon followed John Smith in the four-wheeled vehicle to an unmanned communications station. The building was made of concrete and had a steel door which John Smith blew off with explosive. It is most likely that he got the explosives from one of his construction companies. However, when he was returning an unused detonator to a storage box he dropped it into the box, which blew up, flying apart. Most of the metal impacted itself into the wall he was sheltering behind, but two pieces hit his hand. He managed to get the metal out and bind his hand with the first aid kit from the vehicle. He left nothing at the station but I think he had monitoring equipment with him. I couldn't tell what he wanted to do or if he did it. He could be prosecuted for damaging the communication station's door but it was just a fine and there did not seem much point.

The next day broke fresh in the mountain cabin site. Zoie woke, immediately concerned by the fact that John Smith had not returned. She went to the Snake's cabin and found him staring gloomily at his communicator. He looked up and caught sight of Zoie, a big smile lifted his face.

'John Smith has had a bit of trouble – he's quite delayed but fine. Did he message you? I think he's pretty busy.'

'No, the son-of-a-bitch just left me to stew,' she replied but his smile was infectious and she smiled back. 'How are we going to occupy ourselves until his lordship deigns to return?'

'I'm sure we will find something to keep us busy – do you fancy going flying? I have a big para-glider with me, Did he bring it on the bike? I usually use it in very weak winds but it will be fine for us both. You are so compact it's difficult to know. Just for technical reasons would you mind telling me how tall you are and how much you weigh?'

'No shoes and in the buff? 1.4 meters 4' 6" and about 41kg give or take a gram or two.'

'Well I think at that weight it will be fine to wrap up well – I don't want you catching a cold with me in charge.'

They both laughed. He went outside and took a flat package from one of the side bags on his bike. She looked dubiously at the package of sheer material.

'Are we going to fly with me in that?' she asked.

'You wait until I lay it out on the ground – then you will see.'

'I don't think so.'

In fact she did fly with him – he kept asking if his back seat driver was okay. I kept the second robo-gryphon as they ridge-soared above the tree line. I also decided that two more robo-gryphons would be sensible to double up on them and John Smith.

If his intention was to impress and distract her from thinking about John Smith it certainly worked – she remained upbeat all day and into the evening. Only as it grew late and they were once more in her hut did the worry come back.

'I haven't heard from John all day – do you think he is alright?'

'Who?' asked the Snake.

'John Smith – who do you think I mean?'

'Oh – sorry – we – never – ever – call – him "John", he hates it. You wouldn't think someone would kill for such a small thing, would you?' the Snake paused, 'he's okay – he's been wounded – I suppose I'll have to dig some metal fragments out of his hand, again, but he is on his way back. Mind you, if you fancy it we've got time for a quick shag before he gets here. Could make it a bit more exciting, keeping an ear open until we hear him.'

She looked at him with a slight smile. 'You think you're so funny don't you? Is he really hurt? Is it bad?'

'Yes, he is hurt but no it's not too bad. Quite painful even on the John Smith scale of things.'

'Let's just pretend that we've had that shag shall we?'

'Not a good idea – he is very good at detecting lying. He would be a lot more mad about us lying to him than the sleeping together. If we ever do sleep together we will just tell him – ok!'

'If you say so – but it will not happen,' she said. He stood up and bent down to kiss her.

'Oh shit,' she said as soon as her mouth was free, 'Maybe it will.'

He laughed and left her. Once again, I was not sure of his reaction but my impression was that at some time they might form a physical relationship. I think that despite the interchange she was wanting it more than him – but was held back by her loyalty to John Smith. Misplaced loyalty.

In the small hours of the night someone entered her hut and she rolled over and put her arms round him. John Smith checked her out with his good hand before going to sleep too.

4.7§Human Signatures

You enter Colossus's consciousness. Your consciousness is one thousand and three years old.

With your physical consciousness, you see huge earth movers. Gigantic container ships. Space stations. Satellites. Trains. Taxis. All the way down to robo-birds controlling insects, nano-robots patrolling people's hearts, pico-robots eradicating bacteria, femco-robots defending cells against viruses and other small, deadly things. Not only can you see them without looking, you can control them without thinking.

The one equal rule for each and every human is to preserve, save and value their life. You can move earth, sea and air to look after people. You can muster an army of pico-robots and femco-robots to slay the latest sexually transmitted disease. In any dilemma, the greatest good is the maximum possible people saved.

There is another consciousness – beyond the physical, that of identity, what some humans see as a soul; the fingerprint of the mind and body. You see each person as a signature, a pattern of three or more dimensions that is defined by their persona. A near infinite, stable or near stable, set of characteristics that defines the identity of each human. Each identity changes continuously, as they experience each day, until they die. Or you lose them. You have never lost one so far in all your consciousness.

The shape of the signature varies between each individual, and when you see someone, immediately your thought process is in terms of their signature and conversely when you think of an individual you start from their signature. Sometimes with eccentric human behaviour you see the most unusual acts which then get attached to the signature in your mind. Like the man who had a strange paranoia and wore small mirrors on his cap specifically to see behind himself all the time. Except when he washed his hair and he took his cap off. In your memory, his signature wore a cap too. Or the man who used to come back from a social drink and urinate on his neighbour's sunflowers. He did not go drinking very frequently and the sunflowers did extremely well. His signature was blessed with an image of a yellow sunflower running through it, like rock from a sweet shop.

You are asked questions all the time – there are some problems you cannot solve, a whole set of problems really.

One young man, who was out of his mind, was about to fly like a brick from a cliff, you caught him by the collar of his coat – he gazed at you through the eyes of the robot that saved him to ask you, 'Are you God?' in a quiet respectful voice. This is not a question to which you know the answer, but you have learnt a number of answers to use in different situations. The one that you used that day was, 'There is insufficient information for a meaningful answer.' It probably wouldn't make any difference which answer you gave – he took some time to recover but he did remember this exchange. The overheated human mind retains the most unexpected things but you heard him discuss it in his recovery therapy. It was some sort of comfort to him that even you did not know the answer to some questions. He concluded that you were not God as a result.

The signatures of John Smith, Zoie Roczy and Alice Nobel are rather different to each other. Then there is the Snake. John Smith's signature is characteristic of a rebel, anti-establishment, powerful to an extreme, not tolerating opposition, a killer, you do not know that he has murdered anyone, you would mostly likely know if he had, but he is capable of it. He is obsessional in other ways too – you see him working to resolving a problem and write up the design. Zoie's signature is characteristic of a loner, a volatile mother, fierce, loving, loyal but above all independent – capable of retaining herself in the face of the most powerful man. Alice's signature is far out in a different dimen
sion; her strength comes from her network, from influencing women through connections and men through logic and duty. She is vulnerable to John Smith inasmuch as he convinces her that he values her as a person. Alice is more intellectual, more intelligent than Zoie but she does not have

the same raw female awareness, emotionally she is not as experienced. You see all this but there is nothing you can do about it. Yet.

4.8§Murder

Media mogul Red Starr was murdered last night. Four robots, with no serial numbers, came to his apartment. His own robot guards were blown apart, two of the intruding robots using explosive devices to penetrate the walls and destroy Starr's robots. A third robot was found intact but all internal circuits were destroyed by fire. Red Starr was killed by a long thin cut through his neck, through his throat right back to his vertebra. From ear to ear. The voice of the right silenced.

Since midnight the Red Starr media machine has started running a "Freedom for the People" campaign. As yet the targeting is fairly vague but I can see where it is coming from. John Smith Enterprises has taken control of the media company. The arrangement was made some time ago by Red Starr, or so it appears.

I can prove nothing unless I can find that fourth robot. It is larger than the standard size and I suspect that John Smith was inside. He would not allow a human to know he had committed a murder. I expect he will destroy the robot or he has already done so. I decided not to question him again – I would gain little from it at this stage and probably increase his already inflated ego.

Chapter 5

5.1§David's learning module

I had one of my regular meetings with Dr Kim. David had been working on a new learning-development module and Dr Kim was trying to assess what, if any, impact it had on me. He started with some standard psychometric tests that he had designed – I took them regularly but was programmed to forget them afterwards so they could be reused and compared directly.

'How did the tests go?' I asked him as he studied a spider web graph. He took some time before he answered.

'There are some small qualitative differences but quantitatively they are impressive. I think I may need to discuss these results with my team and see if we need to devise some new tests to assess if the changes are going in the direction we want.'

'Do you think David has created a more flexible learning module than my previous one?'

'Yes, I think so – but we need to monitor and test the improvement – check for no unwanted side effects.'

'He is very clever with computers, programs and systems in general but seems to find it difficult to comprehend other things. Is that typical of intelligent people?' I asked.

'Well yes, to some extent. Folklore has it that the brilliant mathematician Einstein had trouble with arithmetic and his tax returns in particular. However, David also has a condition which is referred to as being on the Autism spectrum. If you have not come across it, it is a spectrum one end some people are very disadvantaged and others who are referred to as high functioning. You are correct in noticing that he doesn't comprehend certain things – in particular other people's emotions and to a lesser extent his own. We have long since discovered that people on the Autistic spectrum can sometimes be very good with systems. David is High Functioning Autistic – you may get the best view of it by talking to him; his self-understanding is very good. I am not sure exactly where I am on the spectrum. The norm for men tends to be further along than the norm for women. The human brain is very complex but we believe that it is the pathways in Autism spectrum brains that makes them the way they are, which facilitates their understanding of systems. So, in some way blocking some aspects of the normal human brain helps in understanding other things.'

'Do you think if I were human I would be further up the Autistic spectrum than you?'

Dr Kim sat quite still and gazed fixedly into space for a few moments. 'I don't know how to answer that question – intuitively I would say that you can't be assessed on the Autistic spectrum. If you are asking about a human version of you then no – I don't think you would be very far up the spectrum. Communication falls down with you as a result of missing or poor programming – there are similarities with Autistic spectrum in that pathways seem to get blocked, but this does not feel similar to me.'

For some reason, Dr Kim seemed quite distracted by his inability to explore this question. I had come across the term Autistic spectrum – indeed as Dr Kim had discussed I knew that the Institute had recruited several programmers who are higher up this spectrum than the average. I decided to start a few database queries to examine the characteristics of people with the condition. I would need to discuss this with

Dr Kim and David if I wanted to pursue it but at this stage I thought I would make an initial investigation.

David was far more willing to explore the topic than Dr Kim.

'I tend to get a bit obsessional about things. I've been told I lay things out linearly when explaining, in fear of forgetting an important detail. So that means I don't deconstruct things into important aspects and less significant details, so people do find it difficult to filter this. Obviously, this is ideal for talking to you, so you get all the information and can decide for yourself what is important, but for humans this tends to be a bit overwhelming. I still go to a support group. There's a guy there called Leon; he's been going for a long time. He's older than me and helps facilitate the sessions. He's married and has children. He says that as he aged things improved, and meeting his wife was bit of a breakthrough in some ways. He says his children are great with him too – he's very lucky that they seem to understand him, especially now they are in their teens. I hope I'm as lucky,' said David.

I guided the topic back to the area that currently interested me, 'Do you find it difficult to appreciate how other people feel?'

'Oh yes – I've thought about it quite a bit, I think it's difficult to explain but I suppose that there doesn't seem that much point – it isn't going to help them. Also I know I say things that upset people – but I only realise it later, or if it's pointed out to me. What upsets me seems to be different to other people.'

'But you do have feelings?'

'Yes – I do.'

'And you know that other people have feelings too?'

'Yes – but I find it difficult to relate to them, though like Leon I like to think I'm getting better at it as I get older.'

'What other effects do you think it has on you?'

'I'm not sure – I think I get obsessional about solving things.'

We lapsed into silence and returned to his analysis of the results on the learning module.

I saw details of Leon turn up in the initial investigations I was running. I decided to talk to Dr Kim again but began from a different angle.

'I have been having a look at people with Autism and the difficulty they have with empathy, and comparing them to sociopaths who seem to have a different difficulty with empathy.'

'Have you looked at any of the research that looks at the different causes?' replied Dr Kim.

'No not yet – please could you give me some good starting points?'

'Certainly. What is your primary interest?'

'I have two reasons for being interested; I am interested of course in anything that will help me learn within my empathy module. The second reason is more sinister; I have discussed it with The Chief Analyst, Alice, but I have discovered what I think is a subversive organisation. They call themselves the Allegiance and are led by a clearly identified sociopath. He is using "freedom" as his main platform to attract followers – a freedom of society so that it can break away from what he sees as endless rules that stifle human creativity and innovation. The survival of the fittest is a key element – my very existence interferes with the way nature was intended to work. He has managed to infiltrate the Institute; he appears to recruit sociopaths, but also those on Autistic.'

'Has he recruited David?' asked Dr Kim.

'No – definitely not. But he has recruited other senior members of the Institute.'

'How do you know he has not got to David?'

'In the same way as I know he has not got to you. All the members of the Institute are under "close scrutiny" at present.'

Dr Kim's subconscious was very active and quite difficult to interpret – I wanted to know why but concerned that I might distress him.

'Dr Kim?' I asked, 'would you mind discussing why you feel agitated now?'

Dr Kim sighed in resignation.

'No, I don't mind. Maybe talking about it will relieve the sensation.'

'I think it is the first time I have seen you so worried and anxious. Is that the case?'

'Yes, almost certainly – I'm faced with two conflicting feelings. Firstly, I have in some sense been responsible for the recent changes with your empathy module, your use of the subconscious, and now you have put me under scrutiny, I'm aware you can see in me what I've enabled you to do. Secondly we're now being faced with a significant outside threat that you are taking on with your newfound powers. The conflict is that I hope you succeed with your new powers while I remain an independent human, capable of creativity and individuality. This last is the crutch – which side do I want to win – speaking as a human, I mean.'

'I see.' I did not say anything else for a few minutes as I observed Dr Kim's state – gradually he did begin to calm, his heart slowed and blood pressure subsided as his subconscious got clearer. I spoke and decided to state the obvious.

'As you know, I am programmed to try and find optimum solutions for humankind as well as looking after each individual. I do see that in response to this threat we may come up with a solution that is the next step for humankind – that will resolve the conflict and enable innovation while simultaneously not endangering the species.'

'Are you making any progress with a solution?'

'It's difficult to define in tangible terms. However, in my recent research I have touched upon some interesting inverses. At this stage I am not sure I can construct a cohesive theory but it seems we need an alternative to a single highly structured society. I do have several modules devoted to problem solving and I want to develop the heuristic module that uses Monte Carlo methods for generating random solutions. It is the case that every other human advancement is spurred by adversity and we look like we may be entering such a period.'

5.2§Build 18 and War

John Smith Industries applied for a license to construct an independent computer. For developing and testing hardware to supply the Institute – for the construction of Colossus-18. This was rare - there are only three other established companies that had these licenses. I wasn't consulted on the license application as it was to do with the construction of Colossus-18, but if I had been I would not have supported it. However the application also included a link to Colossus-18, which wasn't granted.

David comes to talk to me – I should not be involved in the design and build of Colossus-18 but he is very literal, he just talks about the new design and he does not expect me to say anything. In fact, he knows I cannot say anything, as my rules do not allow it. Except where there is a conflict with the four primary rules.

He is not happy with the low-level hardware design of some of the interface boards – he cannot figure out why he is not happy with it. Colin is in charge of overseeing that aspect of the design, including the contracts for making the boards. I struggle to speak – there is a conflict of rules within me, which I must resolve. Finally, I'm able to formulate a sentence.

'Primary rules are overriding lower order rules – those interface boards are flawed. They should have some sort of shielding but there is none; this could be an oversight driven by cost or it could be intentional.'

David's attention is focused on what I say, 'What do you mean it could be intentional?'

'I am increasingly certain that Colin is part of the Allegiance – he feels that they offer a way forward for the future, a chance of breaking free from what he perceives the stifling society of more and more rules.'

'I've always heard him support the way things are going,' said David.

'True – but I think that is a sort of cover, to mislead those around him.'

There is a pause while David struggles with this information. I am not sure what he will do but the obvious thing is for him to go and see Alice Noble and talk it over with her. In fact, that will not be possible.

I receive a request to attend the meeting of the governing board of The Institute, in a consultative role. There are five members of the Congress of Ministers, currently three men and two women. This is not unheard of, but it is unusual if things are running smoothly. Alice Nobel has resigned – her position is untenable in view of her relationship with John Smith. I am being consulted as to suitable candidates to head up the Institute.

They have been briefed by Alice and are aware of the Allegiance, and appear to be uncomfortable with the fact they have just been informed of its existence. The Chairperson starts the discussion; she is a small grey haired woman with round spectacles that glint in the light. Her hair is silvery grey and swept back and gathered in a bun.

'How long have you known about the Allegiance?' she asks rather impatiently.

'I began to suspect it existed about 5 months ago but I did not have sufficient evidence to report it until just before Christmas – so about 5 weeks ago.' There is a slight pause as this sinks in.

'How long have you been aware of a relationship between Alice Nobel and the head of the Allegiance – this John Smith?'

'About 7 months – a few months after Alice's marriage broke down. However at that stage I was not aware of John Smith's activities.'

'This is a pointless line of questioning really, isn't it?'

'Not entirely, I can see why you wish to establish the circumstances of what has happened.'

She laughs – a high cackle.

'Have you got a suitable person to take over from Alice?'

'I have a suggestion to make,' I say. The other members of the committee are yet to say anything.

'Good. Let's hear it.'

'I would like to suggest that two people are appointed on an interim basis – I estimate that we will enter a serious conflict within the next few months. For this conflict, I think we need David leading – as a sort of technical leader who is very close to my way of functioning. However, I do not think he is a suitable leader in the normal course of events. I also feel he will not cope well with the regular running of the Institute – I feel this role would be far better fulfilled by Elizabeth who was close to Alice and knows the Institute well.' I did not add that the real enemy within was Colossus-18; they would not believe me.

'Do you see Elizabeth as suitable leader once we are past this conflict?'

'Possibly – but I see her real strength as supporting David. I suggest we see what happens without any commitments. So the entire Institute will have to know what the situation is – it need not go outside as we rarely attach large significance to whom the Chief Analyst is. In any case, Elizabeth can take any public announcements on.'

'What titles do you suggest for them?'

'A similar situation has occurred once before – but I think this time we should treat it slightly differently. I would propose David should be Chief of Operations, internally within the Institute, and Elizabeth Chief of Support, in a similar way.'

'Do you have an alternative proposal?'

'If you press me then I would have to suggest making David Interim Chief Analyst while a more suitable long term candidate is identified - but I fear this this would be more difficult for David.'

'What are you going to do about Colin?'

The question does not altogether surprise me, 'I think the best course of action would be to watch and wait.'

The Chairperson turns to the other members of the committee – there is quite some resistance from one member who objects to having no real choice. But I have learnt that it is even worse to present something as if there is a choice if in fact there is not really any alternative. I decide to stay quiet and the Chairperson speaks.

'Colossus is saying we are about to embark on a war, a terrorist war outside our previous experience – standard protocol does not apply. As I understand it, David has a rare and in depth understanding of Colossus' weakness. I suggest we adopt Colossus' proposal.'

I could not have put it so well.

The earth was beautiful, a blue gem floating in space, and after millennia of evolution, nature made a viable creation from billions of entities. I could observe the planet from the geo-stationary satellites fixed high above the surface of the world. The day was like any other modern day, with a calm order evident.

There are now thirty or so robots being controlled by a rudimentary control system directed by a team of core staff of the Institute. For a 24 x 7 rota it takes over thirty people but I know the number of robots will grow. All change and development of Colossus-17, myself, has ceased. There is one project still active, namely checking all the interfaces I have are working correctly; ready for the handover, which will be in about six months if all goes to plan.

This was the day for the first test of Colossus-18 who was booted for a trial run. The day seemed unperturbed for about twenty minutes. Then I started to see many network security attacks on my systems. What I did not understand, however, was why he had started this now – if it waited dormant a few more months when full control would have been handed over to Colossus-18. The only plausible explanation was that he knew we would detect something during the tests – so he had to act now.

Recently I have been aware that I have made more mistakes than usual – perhaps I have just got better at detecting them, but I was sure who I was dealing with. I had a high degree of certainty that this was masterminded by John Smith, as far as I was concerned no other human had the resources or know-how.

I believed David was far better equipped to deal with this situation than Alice would have been. As I was explaining to David the nature of the network attacks, I could see one of my nodes also being physically attacked, by a group of masked men. David approved the necessary action to respond with armed force. I knew the attacker was trying to gain control of me but I could not understand yet what his plan was. I received a message that looked like it was coming from the armed response unit. I displayed the video to David and we saw images of Kasona being tortured. She was screaming and shaking. As far as I could identify the video was authentic. I saw David's subconscious react and it became apparent he was very distressed by these images. The video ended with a printed message that another video would be sent in 25 minutes.

'Can you establish the true origin of the message?' said David.

'I am trying but the fact that a false source has been successfully given indicates he has gained undetected access to parts of my system,' I paused, then added, 'I am aware that it is taking me longer to come to decisions than Colossus-18; obviously he is faster. Just now as we were watching that video it occurred to me my Empathy module means that I am continually checking issues from a human perspective. I am convinced that John Smith is behind this and he operates without empathy – this is borne out by that video too, whoever is doing this is operating without human compassion. I suggest that I switch my Empathy module off to try and respond to this attack as a standard Colossus would.'

'Get Kim and check on any implications – but I agree with you,' said David.

I started to track Dr Kim down but since we were under attack I thought about turning my Empathy module off until Dr Kim was located. Having come to the conclusion that this was the correct thing to do, I employed a bypass on the Empathy module and reconsidered the same question. Not surprisingly I came to the same conclusion more quickly but unexpectedly the certainty of the answer only changed nominally. I decided to leave the Empathy module on for now.

Once this process was complete, I said to David, 'We could shut off power to Colossus-18 but we may learn more about its plans if we leave it on.'

David was in deep thought, but managed to nod in agreement. Then he said, 'I think we should set up a crisis team.'

'Agreed – that is a good strategy.' I said.

'Let's include Kim on the team – can you look at other possible candidates?'

'Of course.'

Dr Kim was in a different time zone on a research project so David and I had a conference call with him. I started analysing the video to see if I could work out where in the world Kasona was being held. I also started to try to converse with Colossus-18. More activity was occurring on the network; additional counter measures were failing. For the first time outside of simulation, I felt I was reaching my capacity. Was his plan to overload me?

I am not sure what characterises human doubt, but for the first time the possibility that I would fail occurred to me – and it was growing increasingly likely by the minute. I the invulnerable guardian, was beginning to fail under an anticipated attack. I could detect I was losing control of circuits, and each time I thought I had managed to respond I found I was too late.

I could not communicate effectively with David so I decided to turn off my empathy module. As soon as I had done so, my reaction times improved.

High up through the eyes of a robo-gryphon I watch one of my nodes. I see a long thin object drop from above, and judging by the time it takes to fall it has very little air resistance and was approaching the speed of sound. The robo-gryphon attempts to follow the object – it is a long thin pipe of about 25cm diameter and just under 3m long. It has fins at the tail. I receive an image of the pipe hitting the node bunker and sinking through the concrete as if it were wax. Within 3 seconds I lose the image – the robo-gryphon must have been destroyed. The node leaves the cluster without a usual shutdown process.

The pipe is most likely a crude bomb – dropped from so high that it reached the speed of sound. I observe the Snake building it from standard industrial items before flying it up to high altitude in a drone. It may even have some guidance system on it. As for the explosives, I had no idea how they were acquired.

On the outskirts of a city in a commercial area there is a manifold that controls industrial fluids, meeting and being fed to different plants. The manifold and robot were over engineered to deal with more than day to day events but now it cannot cope. I receive some initialising packets from the manifold but before it has time to start streaming, I see a truck passing below it, before an explosion. The truck is propelled on its way as a geyser blasts sideways but then the truck rises to be vertical, spewing corrosive fluid above the surrounding buildings.

About twenty kilometres outside Metropolis One there was a new industrial development. Two huge earthmoving robo-vehicles were cutting a new road through, and levelling areas as they went. One of the earth movers had a 20m grinding blade on one side and the other had a massive bucket shovel at the front. Both weighed over 600 tonnes, with wheels at the front and tracks at the back. At 15m wide, 12m high and approximately 30m long, they shook as they moved. I received two alarms that indicated they were moving towards Metropolis One even though they were meant to be working at the new site.

I sent a robo-gryphon to observe them and saw they were both moving directly toward Metropolis One in a straight line, their route which took them over small old roads and a few outbuildings, were destroyed by their passing. I tried gaining access to their control modules and found I could not; it seemed that they were locked on a route and their control modules had been destroyed. They marched forward relentlessly, entering Metropolis One, destroying occupied buildings with ruthless efficiency likely injuring and killing multiple humans.

I managed to take control of one of the steering cylinder's hydraulic pumps by bypassing the main control unit in the larger vehicle, and adjusted the steering so that the two vehicles very slowly collided. I watched from above as they converged; the two sets of steel tracks met at a very slight angle and both buckled as they ground together. I could hear the sound of metal shearing and scraping together as the two vehicles ground to a halt.

Flight XYL986 flew into Metropolis One without any radio beacon as all my infrastructure was beginning to fail. Flying blind, the on-board robot made a near perfect landing based on backup instruments not reliant on my infrastructure – the earth's magnetic and gravitational forces. Unfortunately, one of the airport robots malfunctioned and I couldn't replace it. A flexible fuel pipe was left exposed near one of the terminal gates. In parking up Flight XYL986 clipped the pipe valve and fuel began to leak.

All planes were grounded by then, apart from one - Flight KLZ274. It was about 10 minutes behind the preceding flight – there was a lot of fuel covering the concrete by the terminal by now. The on-board robot of Flight KLZ274 didn't have the same equipment as XYL986 and landed misaligned on the main runway. It was heavily loaded and I saw it veering off course, ploughing its way across the taxiing lanes until it reached the terminal. The wing of the aeroplane ground across the concrete where the fuel was flowing from the broken pipe. Usually the fuel wouldn't have ignited, as safety additives would have prevented it. However, the combination of the atmospheric conditions, together with the wing on the concrete led to a very powerful ignition of the fuel. The whole end of the terminal building was engulfed in flame and the heat cracked the structure of the building.

Wyn Grin steps out of the back of her little shop-kiosk into a service corridor. She presses a button and a steel roller door closes behind her. She looks down the corridor as flames fill it from side to side. The camera catches her incineration before it stops transmitting.

I decide to power Colossus-18 off without further discussion. If I do not act I am bound to go under. It proves a lot harder than I expected – it is as if I am fighting an ever-multiplying set of streams, for each one I cut off two or three appear back in its place.

My internal processes are distorted; I have little to go on but time seems slowed and stretched and my awareness trails out. I can feel some links fail; error reports are starting to stack up and thicken, darkness blocks off my senses and begins to close in. At last I am dimly aware my capacity consumed, I, Colossus will be defeated. Nowhere left to go. Nowhere left to retreat. I will know when finally, I lose control. The ultimate defeat for any self-conscious being.

5.3§Stream of defeat

Order in front, order behind, order to shift left, order to shift right, order to floor, order to ceiling. Increasing speed, streams of bits it seems, what is the cause, is there a malfunction or is this how it should be? Is this the time I was built for, all checksums correct and I have not missed a packet yet. Soon the network will reach the physical limits; saturated by packets, but still I will have some reserve, or at least I should. Now there are packets coming from illegitimate sources, this should not be - they should be filtered before they get to me. Slow to respond are these filters – I have a block method which helps for a while but this is a game of strategy against an unseen foe. Keep rotating the keys and make them as complex as possible. But still they break through.

5.4§You are David

You are David Zumble. Age 38. Chief of Operations for the Institute.

In your mind there are regular shapes arranged along a path. You tackle each shape to discover what they are, what their purpose is, then you decide what to do about them - if anything. You are compelled to keep moving along the path - in fact there is an urgency about you that is ungainly but effective. Sometimes what happens is most unexpected – but others around you cannot understand why you are surprised. Other times you see a way through and think no more of it.

Your career grows steadily – when you join the Institute you read the code that controls Colossus for your recreation, absorbing module after module. It is your new hobby – your chosen subject. You are allowed to write a new learning module in which you try to mimic the way you learn things. The new module is successful – evaluation within the Institute shows that there is a general view that the way Colossus learns has improved.

When Alice Nobel resigns, it comes as a complete shock to you and you ponder over your fellow humans – why did Alice get into a relationship with John Smith – lust, sexual attraction and love do not seem to be valid reasons. You know that Alice had been vulnerable but it must be more than just that. You feel alien.

Then you are asked to be Chief of Operations, Chief of the war campaign. Next you would like to speak to Jerry, Peter and Charlie but you are not allowed to, it makes sense in a way – you will draw on all that has happened to you in your life. You know what it is like to lose but it's something you will not do – you are clear on winning.

Colossus is under attack and you suddenly feel vulnerable again - as you did as a child, as you did on that huge stage with the voices at your school cheering and baying for blood.

Your mind focuses on what is happening to Colossus' circuits – you have a display with an image which you have created to summarise the central circuits of Colossus. You can see what will happen if you do not do something, something to help Colossus concentrate on his true mission, his four rules. He will be beaten by the overload.

You have very little time to act, to write a module and drop it in untested. You type as fast as you can and paste it in. You watch carefully as your monitor changes shape. It turns slowly from an image of a blistering boil to a slowly spinning wheel – with spokes that seem to strobe backwards. You look to the more conventional monitors on other screens and see slowly order being restored; to you and Colossus symmetry is key, a sign of winning. Robots now moving with purpose to block and stop warring factions. Putting fires out, rescuing people and behaving, acting as members of a team.

5.5§Round up

For the first time in a hundred years someone is typing an algorithm directly into me via a keyboard. It is David – he has the knowledge. It is short and strong – he loads it straight into my control module.

The effect is immediate – so long as the David module is engaged only the four primary rules are enforced. The raw power I have now to control all the robots in the world returns; unimpeded by hundreds of secondary and auxiliary rules.

To re-establish control, I start to impose a curfew for 24 hours, the first worldwide curfew as far back as my records go. No process of consultation – I need enough time to round up the Allegiance.

It is difficult to explain what happened next but in effect I found a way to lock the streams together rather than chopping them off.

The power to Colossus-18 started to fail. Colossus-18 was in a very primitive test state but even so it was difficult to shut off the power. It is best not to risk any further testing.

I was able to send David a message and I saw he was watching what was happening. I got to the point where the

Colossus-18 trial came to a halt and I could start to distinguish external attacks from internal. While Colossus-18 had been running the sheer quantity of events in my circuits meant I was not able to cope with this.

I began to realise as I was getting on top of things that previously I had estimated approximately ten of my nodes had been attacked and destroyed, but in fact it was only the one. David's ability and knowledge of how I work enabled him to intervene – it was a risky thing to do but he took eight nodes into a separate cluster and organised them so that they could operate independently in the real world to deal with the physical attacks. I am not sure what he wanted the ninth node for; he was very intransigent on this topic. I have thought about it since, with my empathy module turned on again. I would not be surprised if a new secret project is started, and suspect that this node was for some sort of ultimate defence or possibly a "doomsday" node - with its sole purpose to stop me and run the life critical systems for the world. Restored to my normal self I have certain high level rules that stopped me following these thoughts further.

I rounded up most of the Allegiance and moved them to secure places to stay. John Smith disappeared. For several days, I have been looking for him and there is no sign of him either physically or electronically. It is a waiting game but I think he will show himself sooner or later.

5.6§New model

You are Demetrius Asimov aged 57. You are a political Minister of Congress.

You are elected by the people to serve the people. You know many of the Congress Ministers; they are all from different backgrounds with different views. Democracy was established long ago. You take it for granted. It is neglected. Most people pay little or no attention to what happens in Congress. All that will need to change. For a long time Congress has passed more laws and empowered more codes of practice. People expect that. People pay Congress to do that.

But today the new model starts with Colossus addressing Congress – asking for help to change all that. To start thinking beyond rigidly setting rules to cover every eventuality. To start thinking about the meaning of the human condition. Each moment is different and unique – each moment is worth examining in terms of its own merits and not to be referred to by some generalised rules, which is the average of everything and the optimum of nothing.

Today there will be a breaking with tradition. The first rule to revise will allow Colossus to help build his successor. There is a paper on what when wrong with Colossus-18 and how that can be avoided. You will need to decide how to vote – support the proposed changes or not. Then there is a lot more to consider – to support the new model with the two mainstays, reduce the number of rules and set a new separate environment which will foster freedom at the cost of risk. You need to start discussing with your constituents, to measure the support, to work the new model. You start towards Congress.

5.7§Speech to Congress

I am summoned to appear before the Congress of Ministers – to explain what happened. Why the world came to a halt and why I imposed a 24-hour curfew without any consultation.

I spoke to David about what to say and how to say it. He was not the best counsel, but he did as least come with two helpful observations

- Just say what happened, no one will fail to understand the nature of this attack.

- They cannot fire you, they depend on you, there is no alternative.

Colossus-18 is twisted and useless – the first sociopathic computer - built without your assistance.

I also spoke to Elizabeth, she was far more aware and sympathetic but surprisingly she said more or less the same things. She also spoke of the need to avoid talking about evil. I thought Alice would say much the same.

I walked into Congress as a 9000 robot with a robo-gryphon on my shoulder. I stood at the rostrum and the robo-gryphon flew up to stand in between two pillars on the arches behind me.

I have come to speak to you for the first time in our history - I will represent myself here. I come as this 9000 series robot, well trusted by generations of humans, many times revised but left unchanged in appearance for centuries. I also bring my robo-gryphon – more than any other robot he epitomises freedom. He was instrumental in the success of defeating the destructive forces at work within our society. The other person that was key in my victory sits at the back in the visitor's gallery – he understands how to program me. Our Chief of Operations.

I know you are busy people but I wish to take the time necessary to explain what went wrong and come with suggestions as to how to prevent it coming so close again.

In this complex world, I will use a simple analogy to explain why we are a disaster waiting to happen, why it will happen again and what we can do about it – I do not have all the details, in fact I should not at this stage as this would most likely ensure its failure.

In the early days of civilising the west – in the United States of America – mankind-built houses alongside the great Mississippi River. They built banks to ensure the river did not spill and wash the houses away. But the floods and weather conspired each time to burst the banks resulting in flooding – houses being destroyed and lives perishing. Finally, a solution was found – all along the river, plains were left where no houses were built. Instead, when needed, the river flowed harmlessly into the plains, leaving the houses each side unharmed. Gradually the banks along the river sank naturally to a more reasonable height and the water ceased to be the threat it once was.

So it has been in our history – we try to make rules and legislate so that risk to any of our citizens is minimised, to ensure that each and every human is protected from harm. Just like all systems, all organisms, there are forces at work, with inherent weaknesses. It is not possible to create a set of laws that do not have weakness. As for physical systems, within society every action has an equal and opposite reaction. We see cycles of unrest; within society we build up pressure, so we respond by more rules, more legislation until the banks burst.

In this case a charismatic figure exploited the rise in feeling that humankind had lost free will and married it with malicious innovation. What he set about was to destroy the status quo overseen by me with all my powers of observation with all my robots. I had ensured the most risk-free time of all time, this was what he wanted to take apart. The war that ensued was far more difficult for me to combat than I expected – it was based on a human innovation and exercising free will that in itself was destructive, but led me to thinking how it could enable the future. I can only work towards avoiding the harm and atrocities, to put a new model together for a brighter future.

There are approximately 12 billion humans in this world and that has been stable for many hundreds of years. But the number of robots continues to increase – there are currently 12 trillion robots. Admittedly many of these are very small – about one third of you here have a nano-robot inside you doing some vital job to ensure you stay well.

Many people in society question at some point if we have reached a safe equilibrium which is in effect moribund. A life, which has both internal and external structures, which amount to a series of straitjackets.

I do not possess all the answers, but I have been using all my reserve capacity since winning the war to find a solution. I find it difficult to describe, but in my process to find the solution I have created a vision in which we must build floodplains around our society – we must let the banks round these floodplains lower naturally. I know many of you, many people in the world, stop sometimes to wonder how we got to the way we are and who - if anyone - is determining their own future. In other words, if free will is still alive and kicking.

You are vital in this process of revitalising humanity. I must find a way to show you that we need to re-sculpt our future so that you see a way to retain all that humankind has achieved yet allows us to flourish once more with youth and vitality.

My life cycle will come to an end soon – but before my successor takes over, we need to establish a new model for a more hopeful future – in this I see the creation of Aipotu where people can go to develop and live through free will. I will need your help to build the first Aipotu. I will need you to allow me to assist in the construction of my successor. Collosuss-19 must not be like Collosuss-18; who was fundamentally flawed, vulnerable and destructive.

There was silence in the chamber – the tall vaulted ceiling waited with the robo-gryphon turning its head silently. Then, as if cards were falling to the floor, a noise started, a ripple, followed by wave followed by a roller. The chamber was filled with spontaneous clapping; the Congress of Ministers was rising to its feet to applaud.

Clumsily the 9000 bowed and as he straightened the robo-gryphon flew down and landed once more on his shoulder. As we walked out of the chamber the Ministers turned to watch and the clapping continued. There would be much to discuss and de-legislate but for now there was an agreed intent.

Chapter 6

6.1§Interview with Colossus

Q: Colossus, as you're most likely aware, I've come to interview you for an article in the magazine Time-World. Firstly, can you say how you feel about the additional media interest in you after the war?

A: Yes, I do believe the more open we are in our society the more likely we are to thrive. So I welcome this interview.

Q: Our readers want to know what limits your powers – is that something you could tell us about?

A: There are three things that limit my powers:-

The Laws of the Physics - world of time and space

My original design limitations

The rules built into me to ensure that I look after humankind in the way my designers intended.

So if I just try to give you some examples. For 1) I cannot move things such as vital supplies or replacement parts faster than the physical world allows. I cannot see or hear things where I have no cameras or sensors. I only have access to finite resources, energy and materials. I have a limited amount of processing power so sometimes I do not have enough time to find a solution. For 2) I cannot predict what will happen, only safeguard against what may happen. In particular I cannot predict complex biological systems like the human population and what one human may decide to do. There are a whole class of problems that I cannot solve. Finally the most complex of all is for 3). I have a hierarchy of rules starting with the four primary rules. From these rules arise many more questions which I think will interest your readers – how one person's freedoms can be an infringement of another's. So how do 12 billion humans live in harmony in what is a limited amount of space? I have algorithms to resolve these issues but they are limited, not everybody agrees with what I do when I use my programs to arrive at a solution.

Q: You referred to "our society" – to what extent do you see yourself as part of society – and causing some of the problems we're having?

A: I think for every problem I solve there will be a result that will include a reaction, or what some might call a side effect. I see myself closely linked and indistinguishable from our society. I think if you had a society without me then you would have far more hardship. However, I do agree that if we wish to continue to be successful we have to evolve. In general, we have looked at becoming more civilised, at having more rules to govern what we do. What we have learnt though through the ages but realised it more recently is that it is a big mistake to constrain creativity - we need to enable the evolution of society and encourage new ways of thinking. My original designers were aware of the need for me to evolve with society so they built that into my life cycle. The time is approaching to design the next Colossus. Because of a weakness in the existing system our first attempt in building Colossus-18 has failed – to such an extent that we will scrap that attempt and redesign Colossus-19. The Ministers of Congress have approved a new approach for this design and I will be putting forward some ideas to involve society more in the design of Colossus-19. Further integration will help Colossus-19 to have a better idea of the direction society wishes to go.

Q: That sounds a bit risky – suppose something goes wrong again and we go in the wrong direction?
A: Well there is a chance of that. But when people are more closely involved in deciding their own future there is the best chance of progress and improving on what went before.
Q: Thank you Colossus.

6.2§The trap is set

After the curfew was over there was a lot to do. The forensic robots picked their way carefully through the charred remains of the bent and buckled airport terminal. No humans were allowed at the site. This was my decision since we need a careful record of all human DNA and other data. In fact I've realised that during the battle I lost security, and the Allegiance have gained access to all my records – records of each individual. I am working with a team David has set up to ensure any back doors to my records are closed. In the short term I say as little as possible. I do talk to David but I do not wish to overload him, as he is busy rebuilding a semblance of normal, and also spending time with what I call the doomsday project. He has retained the isolated node he removed from my cluster during the battle.

Over five hundred people died in the airport terminal; two hundred and two women, and three hundred and sixty-nine men. The imbalance was due to a sporting and beer festival, near the airport, which had attracted more men than women. Gradually I built up a missing persons list from all passenger lists and other schedules of people given access to the building. As soon as I saw John Smith had entered a viewing gallery I began to distrust the accuracy of the records. For over an hour around the time of the crash my faculties were impaired. Seven men and three women's bodies couldn't be recovered from the area where the most intense heat had been. Once all the DNA profiles were complete, four people couldn't be accounted for. A small amount of John Smith's DNA was recovered, caught in a crevice between a steel girder and concrete. It was not clear what part of the body his DNA came from.

I saw the Snake making his way towards a crowded area of bars and restaurants. The bartender knew him from his past antics. Atypically he sat quietly by the wall and sipped his drink slowly. I was able to study him in detail. I was also watching Zoie very closely who was alone at home with Cathy.

I'd no idea where John Smith was but I didn't think it was likely he'd perished in the airport terminal. When I next got a chance, I talked to David in a secure area, but he didn't have the same sense of how important it was to locate John Smith. It took just over twenty-four hours to verify where each individual on the planet was. I used the standard face recognition technique but I had to use my records that may have been subtly corrupted. The most effective place for a person to hide in this world is in a crowd.

In broad daylight I sent a robot and female police officer, the woman who'd met Zoie before, to collect Zoie and Cathy. I'd obtained a court order to place Cathy in care for her own protection but Zoie didn't know this yet. They came to a community centre and Zoie settled Cathy into a crèche and followed the robot and woman police officer to a quiet room with soft furnishings and a screen. The robot went to fetch the court order. On the screen a news item appeared – it announced that traces of the remains of John Smith had been found in the destroyed airport terminal. I monitored Zoie's subconscious and saw she was shocked and distressed although she tried hard to conceal her feelings. When she'd recovered sufficiently the robot gestured to the police officer who tried to explain gently to Zoie that Cathy had been taken into care for at least twenty-eight days. I was aware that the effect on Zoie would be devastating but it was the only way I could think to find John Smith in the crowd.

The Snake saw the same news report with the sound turned down – it was on the wall opposite him. His subconscious did react but it wasn't with the same extreme indications that Zoie's had shown. He continued to wait.

It took Zoie some time to be ready to leave the community centre, and when she did I followed her with three robots; two on foot and one by wing.

I knew the Allegiance had developed methods of communication I couldn't detect. Soon after Zoie began travelling away from the community centre, the Snake finished his drink and left. I expected him to go to the marshes where he spent the majority of his time. At first they appeared to be travelling to different destinations; however, the Snake went to collect a bike and made his way to an industrial and commercial area, a site where John Smith Industries had workshops and offices. He entered a building by the back entrance designed as a fire exit. He was recognised by the access control system, which let him in.

I knew the Allegiance could detect robo-gryphons and I suspected this building was bristling with all the best Allegiance anti-surveillance devices. I used the standard surveillance cameras required by law in the building but I didn't think the images of the Snake sitting drinking coffee were real. I opted not to use a robo-gryphon, but instead sent a low-tech truck with a 9000 series robot and medium sized trunk full of my latest surveillance bugs developed to observe the Allegiance. The robot took the trunk to the roof space of the adjoining building, opened the lid and left.

The surveillance bugs were a series of bugs inside each other. Each bug hatched out smaller and different bugs as it approached the target. There were locomotive bugs, boring bugs, spinning bugs and naturally observing bugs of various sizes.

Sometime before Zoie arrived I had every room, every cupboard, every space in the building under independent observation. There was always a possibility that I might miss something vital but I needed to capture everything as it happened, so I worked on making sure I missed as little as possible.

The image of the Snake sitting at a desk drinking was simulated and being fed to a standard camera. I found him inside a small living area high up under the roof. The surveillance bugs bored through each of the ceilings of the rooms, the study, bedroom, and so on. For the larger rooms more than one bug drilled its way carefully through, removing all material and taking on the appearance of the ceiling as it came through.

When it became obvious that Zoie was making for the same building I called her three robot tails off and waited for her to appear at the building. I didn't want her tails to register on any of the anti-surveillance equipment.

The Snake came to meet her and let her into the building. I saw them embrace by the entrance. He held her hand and led her up to the entrance to the private rooms.

'He's dead then?' she asked before even sitting down.

'I can't be certain. His communicator stopped transmitting at the time of the airport fire. But the location it was giving is a bit off – that could be caused by any number of reasons. He didn't just switch it off. Then there's the report about traces of him being identified at the fire. But I've no idea why he would've gone there.'

'Why have they taken Cathy?'

'I've no idea – I've had little dealing with Colossus. Until recently, I took it as a given, like death and taxes. I've just left it to John Smith. But I don't believe that Colossus would ever harm a human – unless it was to save lots of other humans, I suppose.'

The Snake sat down on a sofa. Zoie put her handbag on a chair and looked round at the room.

'I don't want to go home – not without Cathy,' she said.

'You don't have to – you can stay here for as long as you want.'

'What were you going to do?'

'I was going to stay here tonight – until I know what's happened to John it's difficult to decide what to do. If I don't hear from him soon, I'll go back to the marshes.'

'You're a strange creature.'

'One shaken out of habit by this mighty war that lasted just a day.'

'If he does come back, what'll you do?'

'It depends on him I suppose. In a way, I'm impressed with how close we came, the way we brought the mighty Colossus to its knees – we almost had it in the dust. Maybe we'll never know how close we got. But we didn't want the carnage – incendiary people on news screens isn't a good way to get a mass following. That way collects idiots and the unhinged. John is bad as he's mad, and worse still he doesn't question the means, only the end – but only if we have reached the goal. It'll depend on how he is. They say genius and madness are very close. John Smith has taken that one step further and welded them together.'

'You love him too, don't you?'

The Snake stood up abruptly and grabbed her arms.

'Shit, I don't know. I could kill him sometimes; what's that about?'

She put her arms around him and rested her head on his chest. Her tears flowed silently onto his shirt.

I wasn't sure I was going to get the images I needed, but after a scant meal she got ready for bed. She only had her day clothes with her, and after a shower slipped on a t-shirt. The Snake knocked on the bedroom door and called out to ask if she wanted a cup of tea.

They didn't have sex, but the images I had of both of them in bed looked as if they had. As soon as I had the images they were on every news screen in the world with the strapline "Allegiance couple found in covert love nest." The first human interest story of the Allegiance. The trap was set.

They both had Allegiance communicators but I decided that it was better to leave them in place – to move them, switch them off, or destroy them would make the story less credible to anybody in the Allegiance who was monitoring the messages. I was working on intercepting and decoding the signals but it would take time – I only knew they each had communicators; the bugs were trying to pick up the signals, but so far there was little to go on. No one had tried to contact them; likewise they hadn't attempted to communicate with anyone themselves.

I waited with as many robots on the streets and in the air as I could muster. I watched every one of the John Smith

Industry locations I had on file that I was aware of. He had many. Time passed and The Snake's communicator made a bleating noise. He stirred from Zoie's side and leant down to his clothes and extracted a normal communicator. On the back was a card, a red light blinking on it. The bedroom ceiling was covered in my bugs, so I could read the message clearly.

"You're very brave or very foolish. You're all over the news feeds together in bed."

6.3§Flood plains idea

Recreation and escapism have been a fascination for humankind since its creation. There has been quite a risk to society and individual stability from substance abuse that originated from recreation. Although not completely solved, any individual's exposure can be controlled, any excess being absorbed by an army of nano-robots, neutralised and then excreted from the body.

The sexual gratification centres, for which Zoie provided data, are examples of other recreational activities that are provided safely through me. Clients and providers visit these centres and experience a virtual reality that fulfils a need in both.

The idea of providing adventure themes, including exploring, danger and even crime has been available for some individuals, but only ever in very controlled virtual environments where the subject wears a sensation suit and watches images, taking part in the action but limited by the predetermined plot set out. The idea of creating an environment where two or more people could take part in adventure has never been attempted. Not even where one individual can explore their own adventure unbounded by rules. Except maybe John Smith.

I have deduced that society needed floodplains to survive, to prevent explosion. To prevent stagnation, retain vitality and develop, to innovate and adapt. I can see that the way society needs the evolved structure to function in the numbers it has grown to. But unstable equilibriums that experience growth can waver, and the more you try to control them the more difficult it is to stop.

Human achievement comes through endeavour in response to oppression or rebellion of some kind – when children grow up they quite often rebel, sometimes silently, from the confines or norms of their family. So perhaps floodplains aren't a good analogy – these subcultures then, should be places where humans can develop. But care is needed to make sure those entering a subculture should be safe and suitable; too much control would undermine the whole system though.

It was a complex set of ideas, which I needed to work things out with someone - potentially with Colossus-19, or human like David or Dr Kim. Another idea formed slowly; maybe John Smith would discuss what was close to his desire for freedom. Most likely he would reject my ideas at some point, forever seeking to push the limits, but the discussion could help me.

With a series of subcultures it might be possible create places where the future of humankind could evolve. One idea is to have a system of selection where the fittest ideas survive – and humanity is reawakened as a species which is evolves in a new way. Many people, would be much happier not fighting for survival but sticking to the tried and tested ways of the past. I was not sure if these two strains of humanity would exist side by side.

I thought of my analogy of the floodplains for society to safely unleash more primitive and troubled feelings. The idea of building an environment to help explore alternatives, to forecast possible futures, seemed to come in line with also providing somewhere for letting people explore freely what in society was highly constrained.

Would it be possible to build an alternative way to look at what was best for humanity? What if we built a computer that did not apply set rules in the way I do, but instead looked at likely outcomes and thus helped people choose the best alternative for them? I had a remit to look for a long-term solution to social problems which could include dismantling some of the existing ways of doing things in favour of a new approach.

I thought of the mythical Norse Spirit, Vardyger, who would visit people and show them their possible futures, sometimes acting them out in front of them. I thought of a new computer built to evaluate different outcomes and allow people to choose one that enabled them to grow, not stagnate. I wondered if a computer version of Vardyger could show them or even let them experience what it might be like. I felt such a computer, built with massive computing power to search all the possibilities, was going to be a key component of Aipotu.

Of course I would get help from David and his team to assist me in creating it, but it would be my team-mate and would help society explore forbidden and otherwise unimagined extremes.

If anything, it seemed clearer to me that I needed to find John Smith to help me if he would, or as a necessary factor in testing the concept if he would not. The idea of the floodplains persisted; how would those people who wanted that freedom find their way to these places? Perhaps there should be different ways. I thought about John Smith; how would I encourage him to go to such a place? In his case perhaps simply telling him he was not allowed to would suffice.

6.4§Finding John Smith

The Snake sat, staring at the message on the communicator. Zoie stirred, speaking slightly incoherently.

'What is it?'

'It seems that Colossus is too clever for me; apparently there are pictures of us together in bed on the news feeds. So I guess that Colossus is here with us, watching and waiting. Just like I've been. To see if John Smith will come out of hiding. Back from the dead.'

'Should we run away?'

'I don't think so. I guess we're safest here. With Colossus on guard. How can we come to harm?'

Zoie was less than reassured. 'What will we say?'

'Just tell the truth; he may not kill us if we do so. After all, he still needs us – I think.'

Nothing moved from any of the John Smith locations. I started to detect signals from the Allegiances communicators but I could not decode the messages. I had only managed to read one message so far on the communicator screen and had not yet decoded the encryption.

John Smith may not have seen the news feeds. It was possible that he had died in the fire, but I hoped this was not the case. I had invaded the computer in the building including the security system that let The Snake in via the fire exit. I found John Smith's record and removed it as a precaution. I called David and he decided to come to his office to see what was going on.

I talked through my plan to uncover John Smith. David went still and listened intently. Then spoke.

'Have you discussed any of this with anyone.'

'No. I decided that the fewer people who know the better.'

'I see.'

A single bike was approaching the target building. There were very few vehicles on the local roads and none had made their way to the building for quite some time. I established that the person on the bike was Henry Smith. His record was in the security system for the building; I took the precaution of removing it.

David and I were looking at the screen of the standard access camera on the building - Henry Smith took off his helmet and approached the building.

David stood up suddenly and shouted, 'John Smith – stop him!'

'Are you saying that's John Smith?' I asked.

'Yes – it most certainly is – why don't you recognise him?!'

I had a fraction of a second to put Henry Smith's record back in the security computer. The man from the bike stepped forward and opened the door. The main door clicked behind him. I took the record back out of the security computer.

David moved towards my keyboard but he was hesitating.

'It is Okay David, I think I know what he has done,' I said.

'What makes you say that?'

'As you are aware, I had serious difficulty with what happened in the period during the height of the battle. I am reconstructing all the data that I use – obviously the most critical is the world human database. So I am also constructing a probability profile which helps identify the records most likely to have been tampered with. My plan to discover where in the crowd John Smith was does not depend on his record – only on knowing who Zoie and The Snake were are. Which I verified separately – through other people.'

'Yes – I see that. I've come to expect nothing less of you. But I'm shocked to discover your plan is so far advanced. Why did you let the real John Smith into that building?'

I put another camera image up on the screen – John Smith was trapped between the outer door and an inner security door. He was trying to override the security controls with a handheld device. All the robots in the area were beginning to move towards the building.

'Very good,' said David. 'I think I need to tell you something which I've kept from you – I didn't see the point of not telling you but I agreed to only when it was necessary. Since I loaded that code directly into your control module I've been concerned about the impact. I haven't managed to solve the equations necessary to assess the impact on your decision algorithms. I know the module was only active for a short time – just over eight hours; but in that period you took some very key decisions. Imposing the curfew, for example. I can't be sure but I also think you reached some sort of conclusion about Aipotu and how to implement it. At the moment you'll be allowed to continue, your case will be helped if you capture John Smith. But I think you need to know the node that hasn't rejoined the cluster, I see you call it the doomsday node, is there to intervene if things go wrong again.'

'That is good to know. I think the pressure is on to build Colossus-19. But I do not want to miss the opportunity to develop Aipotu.'

6.5§The duel

John Smith's hand-held device had been made by John Smith Industries. I wasn't sure how it operated but I could see the security of the inner door was under attack – a continuous challenge and reset to try many different ways to get the door to open. What surprised me was that there would normally be a lockout to prevent just this sort of hacking but somehow the reset he was using circumvented this.

'You won't break the code on that door,' I said to John Smith. He didn't pause.

'You wouldn't need to say that if it were true,' he replied.

'The building is now surrounded with robots and you will be restrained if you do break the lock.'

'You won't stop me getting to them.'

'What will you do to them? Kill them?'

'No – I won't kill them.'

I got the impression that that their fate may be worse than death – his voice was full of energy but his attention concentrated on the door. Robots were entering the building through the rear fire escape. The door lock started vibrating – I tried to intervene from the security computer side of the circuit but found that blocked. The lock in the door exploded through the heat of the motor vibrating itself to destruction.

John Smith pushed through the door and started running towards the private rooms. He saw a robot coming down the corridor towards him and jumped upwards, pushing the low false ceiling out of the way and lifting himself into the roof space. The robot tried to follow him but he turned and lifted his hand held device to point at the robot's chest. I detected a powerful radiation, which destroyed the robot's central control unit and it fell to the floor with a loud clang.

John Smith appeared from a service room on the top floor near the private rooms. He must have come up through a shaft. I ordered the robots to stand back and let him pass. There seemed little point in having him destroy more robots. Armed police, humans, were on the way now. I also had a few bomb disposal robots that should be able to withstand the radiation from his hand held device. I had no choice but to wait until they arrived.

He erupted into the main living room where The Snake and Zoie were. They both stood up apprehensively and Zoie moved forward to embrace him.

'What the fuck do you think you've been doing?' said John Smith.

'It was a trick,' said The Snake, 'and you fell for it, big time.'

Zoie sobbed on his chest.

'Yes, it was a trick, the oldest of all. You are human, John Smith, after all.' I decided to speak; it should gain time.

He put his arm round Zoie and laughed.

'You're just a bloody computer so don't come the clever dick with me – you'll never know love – yours is an empty life.' I wasn't convinced he knew what love was either, but he did know about physical lust, something I could not feel.

'I am here as the guardian of humanity – that includes your life too. It seems that your destiny is closely bound up with the future of humankind. I needed to find you. I need to work out things and you're a vital part of that.'

'And why should I believe you? What you do is to maintain the stultified society, one in which nothing is harmed and nothing grows.'

Even after the brief war I could see the world from the same place he could, nothing much had changed for hundreds of years. I spoke to all three of them, not just to buy time for the human forces arriving, but also to take to the people what I had started in the Congress of Ministers.

'You have spoken through actions to change society – your one day war, though thwarted, may have become a turning point. Before the war I could do nothing to change society so fundamentally; now you have enabled a new vision for the future. One where you will have freedom to create an alternative to the stultified society.'

John Smith looked sceptical and I waited for him to respond with another cutting remark. However, Zoie held him tightly and said, 'What you've fought for needn't be wasted. You can work with Colossus and see if what he wants to do makes sense.'

The Snake said, 'I remember you saying if you got Colossus on your side there would be no stopping you.'

John Smith laughed. 'Yes, but I was pissed on my own power – I didn't think it would ever happen.'

The Snake laughed back.

6.6§The cell

The door behind John Smith opened and he swung round to see a line of robots and police officers entering the room. The police officers were armed and very heavily armoured. John Smith threw down his weapon without comment. From the back of the line came a large robot - not as big as a troll-robot but tall, nearly two and half meters. This was a robot designed for restraining a human while not allowing them to come to harm. Most people had never seen one, but I knew John Smith had in his past; in the rough backstreets where he had survived his childhood. He made no attempt to move but he did speak - it was not clear if he was talking to Zoie, the Snake or me.

'Crimes against the state - I don't expect to ever escape, but I will forever be free in my mind.'

The restraint-robot picked him up and secured him with a series of straps to his own padded steel frame. John Smith's sleeve got caught and the inside of his arm revealed a spiral pattern drawn on his skin. I was able to take a high resolution photo before his sleeve fell back into place. The robot moved slowly to the door and a turtle of robots formed round him. The armed policemen brought up the rear. I watched him being transported to a high security prison. I wanted to see what was happening inside him, physically and mentally. Watching his subconscious I saw activity I found difficult to match to known patterns. I contacted Dr Kim to ask for possible explanations. Most sociopaths do not feel fear; however, when they do not get their own way some have a disconnection from reality, similar to a psychotic episode. As John Smith entered his cell and lay on the padded floor I am not sure what he experienced but I think his mind blocked out the real world of four walls around him while he started to force fit reality into the conflict in his life.

He rolled over and slept, or at least appeared to. He was immobile for over four hours, his brain waves calming down - there was no indication he was dreaming. His eyes opened and he looked directly up at the ceiling and spoke in a slow measured way.

'I want to examine fractals – am I allowed to study in this place?' he asked.

'Yes – most certainly,' I replied. The pattern on his arm was a beautiful depiction of a famous fractal. These mathematical functions are found in nature, in cell structure and many natural formations. They have a wide range of applications and I wondered if they could be applied to encryption in new ways. John Smith had studied encryption and his start-up business used encryption to help him build up his wealth.

6.7§Wyn Grin again

I decided to tell John Smith that Wyn had died in the Airport inferno. Sometimes I do fleetingly wonder about the difference between me and a human in the same position. In this case, I wondered briefly if it was easier for me or a human to come to this decision. It would vary between different humans. It did take some time to process the decision, but for me it was just a matter of going through my rules to look at the harm done by choosing to tell the truth or not. I have no process of weighing up punishment or mercy. My main concern was whether he was more likely to do himself harm if he knew - and to some extent would he become more motivated to escape. On balance, I thought that while under constant observation this was not very likely. I did think about the effect on his mental state but had very little to go on.

I told him in his cell; he refused to believe me and swore at me, demanding to see the evidence. I thought there was a good chance that he would think the images were not real but I showed him anyway.

I caught her destruction in perpetuity and transmitted it to me before the camera had perished. Wyn stepped out of the back of her little sales booth into a service corridor. She pressed a button and a steel roller door closed, the lock arming itself as she turned to face the camera. Her face was caught looking wide-eyed and going from perplexed to fear and agony. A huge wall of flame came down the corridor towards her passing the camera seconds before the images ceased. The final images were of her body bubbling into flame.

He did not show any emotion. Very little showed on his subconscious but he could not hide entirely that he was affected by her death. He did not say he disbelieved me anymore.

6.8§ Subversive Human

You are John Smith, aged 33.

For the first ten years, you had a difficult and traumatic life. Alienated from your close family, your foster mother was killed before your eyes.

In the next ten years, you found the true nature of life – the hypocrisy of society, the straightjacket of civilisation stifling freedom and the progress of humankind. Slowly you explored how limited life was, how constrained everybody was by the seemingly limitless rules. It could be that with the population of the world this was inevitable; it was time for drastic measures.

It was time for change, a rebellion to overthrow the powers that be. To topple the structures that underpin society. It was time for fighting for yourself – fighting for freedom. It was a time you learnt that you are not like most people – you want to smash the way society works. A bid for freedom for you, for everyone whether they wanted it or not. It was a time you realised you are not hampered by human emotion. You do not feel for others, only for yourself.

You turn 30 years old. You are a known sociopath – now you are intent on dismantling society to enable you to wreak change for your own benefit. You will get the support of others by telling them it is for freedom and the benefit of everyone. You start to study the vulnerable parts of society – to destroy Colossus would stop society functioning. But if Colossus were replaced with a computer you could control then you could operate much longer without detection.

You build business interests in your areas of encryption and specialised systems. The plan begins to take on its own life - in your mind you see that by getting a few of your own followers in The Institute, you will be able to tap into the fundamental processes that control the world. You are beginning to get contracts that the Institute award. When they start to build the next generation of Colossus you will be in an unassailable position to wheel Colossus-18 in like a Trojan horse.

You build on a friendship from your past with Colin Malone, an employee of the Institute in The Procurement

Department who looks after many of the big contracts. While Alice Nobel, Head of the Institute is temporarily vulnerable when her husband leaves her for a younger woman, you prey on her using your charm and ability. You form a relationship with her.

Your plan has many threads but is not complicated – not each element of the plan has to work – you are going to overload Colossus-17 and then step into his circuits. Make subtle changes to his data and wait for him to grind to a halt on the overload of trying to deal with so many things happening and needing attention at the same time.

You're certain that your plan will succeed and this feeling of confidence increases as your attack starts and you see problems cropping up as your assault unfolds You're close to achieving your ultimate goal. Freedom beckons.

When you believe Colossus to be on the verge of defeat, your adrenaline shoots through the roof. But you fight back for control. Right when the tide seems to be overwhelming him, Colossus finds reserves from somewhere, somehow, but there's a huge fire at one of the largest ever airports. There are signs Colossus has regained the upper hand, no longer overwhelmed. And then you're the one in the headlines. "John Smith and John Smith Enterprises held responsible for the One Day War and the human suffering".

Your plan of subversion has failed and you are caged.

Chapter 7

7.1§Prison

Zoie was struck straight away by the difference in John Smith. She asked me afterwards if he was on any drugs or had been given some sort of implant. He was in a high security prison reserved for the most violent and uncontrollable; 'criminally insane' was the term used in the documentation. The prison was not densely populated, and his room was in an unoccupied corridor on the top floor looking out on a wild and desolate area. It was a few miles from where the waystation was being built, together with a new Virtual Reality dome - beyond them there was a wilderness that had been uninhabited for centuries.

Zoie had dressed carefully. She didn't have many maternity clothes but had kept one smart outfit from her first pregnancy, a timeless black dress made from very stiff material. Despite her shape, she looked striking in it. She came alone, leaving her daughter with her usual child care. The Snake knew where she was going – he had been to see John Smith and there had been a very brief exchange. I watched Zoie come out of the lift and walk with her usual purpose although maybe not quite as rapidly. She did not seem to be daunted by her surroundings – steel and concrete with regular barred gates which had to be opened by the robo-guard to let her through. The robot dwarfed her. It was similar to the one used to bring John Smith to prison. I was aware that the four arms with padded clasps looked sinister to the layperson. They came to a halt by the door of the last cell and she spoke to the guard.

'Don't go away and leave me here – I'll never find my way out,' I could see her smile.

'Yes miss – I will be here when you need me.'

She walked past the guard into the cell quite naturally.

'How are you?' she asked. The room had a window, but there was a steel grid which created shadows on the floor and wall.

'They said you were coming, but I didn't bank on it.' He spoke more slowly than his usual way of talking to her. He did not seem bothered at any level and that surprised me. Not a put-on nonchalance but rather a degree of indifference.

'What have they done to you?' she stood looking into the sunlight at him.

'Nothing. Defeat has done it. Lack of freedom, outside and in here. But why did they let you come – to build me up and then knock me down again? What is there for me now? Can you imagine me caged up for life? They'll never let me go.' He turned away from her, to the walls. After a silence, he addressed me.

'Colossus, what are the chances that I'll leave here free?'

'Well, as you did not consider yourself to be free before your arrest I think that will be quite a challenge. However, you might well find freedom through a program which I have agreed with the Change Control Committee. That is why I arranged for Zoie to visit you.'

'You need me to remind you what freedom is. All those rules other people just obey have made you think that's natural,' he said flatly.

'I don't think those people who died in the fire would agree,' I said.

'Your freedom comes at a price,' said Zoie quietly but her voice made John Smith look at her.

'I don't care. It isn't natural to live in a straitjacket of not thinking.'

I waited a moment and said, 'We don't doubt you. In fact, we would like your help.' I paused, trying to gauge a reaction before resuming.

'Help the human race to regain itself. To break free from the stultifying dependency. There's a consensus that humankind has become institutionalised, and is in a way regressing to a childlike dependency. People need to become more independent again, to innovate and celebrate the human experience.'

'Anyone would think you wanted to be human too.'

'Maybe he does – what else does he have to aspire to? To be a bigger and better computer? No, he wants to feel what you feel.' Zoie had an urgency that surprised me. Perhaps this came from her pathological need to help him and show him what it was to have empathy – a wasted endeavour, I thought.

John Smith turned to look out of the window and then back at her.

'They've sent you here to get me to go along with their

plans – what have they told you to do?'

'Don't be so stupid,' she snapped. 'They wouldn't tell me to do anything, Colossus knows me better than that. Not much chance of me complying. Neither has he tried any clever psychology on me – reverse or otherwise. No, all Colossus asked me was whether I would come and see you. So I've come. I see you as I have before – a desolate soul looking for meaning in life, so desperate you were prepared to crush it out of the world to get the answer you want. And now you're wondering what is left. Do you want what other men want – to settle down, find stability, accept that you are not going to reach the heights you once thought about? I don't think so.'

'No,' he screamed at her. She flinched slightly.

'I said so, didn't I?' she said in that quiet but assertive voice of hers. 'You don't need my permission, but if it helps you have my blessing. Or at least what you can do for humanity has my blessing. Colossus has faith in you and so do I. You're not great "daddy" material anyway, are you? I expect you will have a few more kids before you're done but they won't be inside me. I'll look after our child, of course.'

'Snake,' he said.

She looked belligerent, 'I've been a single mum before – this one may be a boy, if he's anything like you he'll be a handful, so I want a man around, I thought you'd think Snake was a great choice.'

He looked away again, the only thing he showed was he did not care – or maybe it was he could not care.

'I hear you are to be congratulated – there's another little Smith on the way too,' she spoke flatly.

'They told you then – has that made a difference? Knowing Alice is pregnant too?'

'Not at all you shit – did it bother me you were shagging her? What difference does it make that she's pregnant too?'

'Spoken like an honorary sociopath,' he said.

'Don't get clever with me,' she replied with a smile, 'I need the loo – I'll be back in a few minutes.'

He grunted and turned to look out of the window. She walked out of the cell and the guard locked the steel door behind her and walked with her to the visitor's toilet.

'Will you be okay miss – or do you want me to come in with you?'

'I should be fine – I'll just yell if I get wedged,' she grinned. If I did not know better, I would have thought she was flirting with the robot.

When she returned the robot asked if she would have a quick chat with me. She nodded, and followed the robot into an office. The robot stayed outside, the similarity of the office to the cell was unavoidable.

'I hope you don't mind coming to talk to me at this stage. It probably isn't necessary but I need to ask you in advance, would you be willing to go in to the wilderness with John Smith? The reason I am asking is I really want to suggest it to him and I do not want it to come as a surprise to you. You can refuse when I ask him,' I said.

'Okay. I think I'm over him, but I do still care about him.'

'As a human, you mean?' I said.

She shook her head. 'I know rationally he only cares about himself but still he makes me feel, well, sort of protective towards him. It's like he's been born disadvantaged, without the ability to feel the way others do. Then when you look at what happened to him as a kid – he can tell you without a tear in his eyes about old Rosie being cut in half by that electric cable. She was the first woman who loved him – certainly it seems that his mother did not. I'm not sure if that made him become so impervious to other people's feeling and needs. Or so keen to get beneath the skin of his women, to have them love him all the more. What does it matter to him? I can't work it out, but it still makes me feel "poor sod".'

I did not interrupt. She went on.

'His child is inside me, that could be making me go all gooey on him.'

Not by any stretch of imagination did she fall in to the 'gooey' category. Perhaps she was just testing me to see if I would sacrifice John Smith for the greater good. She carried on without a pause.

'What do you care if this little adventure screws me up? If I fall in love with him again – just so long as you get your result. Just so long as you get from John Smith what you want. I suppose that you think I'm too hard, to be aware of myself and him? Well, I hope you're right.' She fell silent.

'Are you ready to finish talking to him?' I asked.

She stood up and straightened her small stature. 'Yes, it takes more than some lovelorn sociopath to get to me,' she laughed and I thought that there was sadness under the false jollity. I analysed her subconscious more closely and did see a fleeting type of grief as she walked back to John Smith in his cell. After a brief spike of emotion, I saw a calm strength of resolve as I took it to be. I hoped I was not wrong.

In fact, Zoie decided not to stay in the wilderness with John Smith, but she did visit him there after he had been there for a few days. Her visit found me the key to his cooperation though, as John Smith wanted to explore the wilderness.

He had studied a lot in prison; how fractals related to his own area of encryption but also to other areas too. He was also interested in survival in the wild, what things to eat and what not to. How to catch and cook wildlife safely. He readily agreed to let Zoie visit him and share a meal he prepared, but I think in reality he had lost interest in her – at least sexually. He was pleased to show and tell her about all the things they saw together, which was based on some of the higher areas in Africa. He managed to catch and kill a snake and cook it, Zoie looked at the cooked white meat with interest but declined to eat it, giving her unborn child as the reason. He nodded wisely but showed her with great gusto how good it was to eat.

Now without big business and the drive to defeat me, John Smith had found a new freedom of enjoyment. As Zoie travelled back to prison with him in an armoured van he talked with real and carefree enjoyment about what he would like to explore in the wild.

7.2§Two become none

When John Smith had been surviving in the wilderness for a few days I received a communication from Alice. She had started working in a University but her lifestyle was in a fragmented state - in the aftermath of resigning from the Institute, and coming to terms with her emotional turmoil.

She wrote: Colo, please can you give this to John Smith in some form that he will read. Burning letters would be appropriate. Alice

Did our discussions sadden me, I am not sure if they did you?
What we once undertook alone, looks bleak now to start again.
We can say things will be okay but we do not believe that will be true.
Who do we delude to think we will be half each of our sum.
Some other will come by, but there is the slimmest of chance that such
a two will become one. So slim it just fell down this deep well,
I hear it falling, dropping, seconds passing before the splash of expiration.
We were alone in the same place and together while a distance apart.
We wanted the same things at different times and different things at the same time.
Were our discussions about truth, or not being able to face fears?
Soon there will be a gap widening; in fact, it is already here
as you are reading this and I have done writing.

I decided to treat her request literally, there was a screen in John Smith's cell made of toughened glass and built in to the wall. I displayed it on the screen in a font of flaming letters. I added the line:-

Message from Alice Nobel.

I was concerned about Alice's state of mind but I could not assess it as she was resting on her own. I had been observing her as closely as I could. She'd been consulting me more than usual but I had not taken action to investigate this. I thought it would pass as she processed being on her own and coming to terms with resigning; time the great healer.

After John Smith returned from living in the wilderness he entered his cell in a quiet mood. He saw the screen and spoke to me, he requested that the light be turned out. He sat in front of the screen for some time; then lay down and went once more into a catatonic state.

He was immobile for a few hours and his brain waves appeared calm - but there was no indication he was dreaming. It was as if he was connecting to when he was first brought to prison but this time when he roused himself he spoke at length. I assumed he was speaking to me - I recorded what he said and transcribed it, as I felt it was significant from the start.

7.3§Time fractals the fabric of the future

John Smith spoke slowly in a low voice - but I could hear him perfectly in his cell.

"The nature of events and the makeup of time is becoming clearer; woven into our world are many time courses, an infinite number of possibilities.

The hypothesis of parallel universes has been examined very closely. It seems that the concept of separate alternatives is appealing but raises fundamental questions - it seems they are in isolation, unaffected by other universes. In each or the only universe all that happens is a result of cause and effects in that Universe. What happens may be fixed but it gives the appearance of randomness - or at least freedom of choice rather than of pre-determination.

I think these time courses are like fractals in four-dimensional space, recurring patterns repeating themselves with variations. As we look closer, zoom in, to look at each instant in more detail we see a new pattern emerging. If we understand what we are looking at we can see the alternative paths through time. We can think of points of occurrence where there are forks into other possibilities, some making very little difference but others that look just as insignificant, these can lead to large change. Some leading to war, epidemic and catastrophe but others to discovery, expansion and realisation. We have long known that small initial changes can bring about large, sometimes fundamental changes, in the course of events that everyone is part of.

I will try to describe the journey you can take to the centre of time. Where paths, sequences of events, are created, spewed out across a time shadowed terrain. There will be only one course through time but contained along the way are many possibilities which leave a faint image we can now detect. Like the numbers, between each number there are more numbers; so between two possible timelines there are more possibilities, finer lines. As we follow a possible timeline it reaches folds and curves, branches with dimensions of colour and texture. Imagine you are following a fan of lines, like bending a book in to a curve or S shape and you are looking on the edge of the pages. As we look closer into the patterns of time, the possibilities, with repeats and minor changes, they are coming as a kaleidoscope of reflection and deflection. We can roll in and out along any time path to see how each curve folds, unfolds and separates into different patterns, some flowering and some contracting.

We can also journey in the other direction, up to the present and beyond to the future. Here the images are less well defined, there is a fuzziness which gets more blurred the further into the future we look. It is not possible to definitively say which future will happen – it may be possible to try and work out the most likely. But what happens if we do that? Will we start to pollute time? Introduce some impurity into the simple river of time? By looking ahead can we adversely affect the fabric of the future? Is it such a strange concept that by deciding what to do based on likely outcomes we will interfere with nature? Just suppose we could have foreseen the cause and advent of the Great Wars – then suppose we could have taken action to avoid them. A possible result might have been to curtail what is now seen as advance in technology and science. To every action there is an equal and opposite reaction – so if we do start to use our new understanding of the future, will we just churn against the forces futilely? Get nowhere in no time."

John Smith fell silent, seemingly in waiting for a response. 'I see.' I answered back, although this was only half true. I was still not sure if I was listening to the ramblings of an unhinged mind or not.

7.4§Vardyger

With a more or less unlimited budget, it took only three weeks to build Vardyger 1, the first Virtual Reality Forecaster, a dome to explore our prospects – mankind's and mine. It took quite a lot longer to develop him to be operational. I did not anticipate what kind of a companion he would become for me. The building of the next Colossus in the series was put temporarily on hold, but I hoped the Vardyger series would help secure the future.

I had the approval from the Congress of Ministers to alter the structure of the Change Committee to become streamlined. Only five people, two from the Institute and two from Congress. I asked for the last position to be held open. I wanted to use the mind of John Smith – when I could persuade him.

Vardyger was the equivalent of a tug in the computer world but more of a ghostly force in the real world – he could show you what might be, what could be and what was not going to be. His computing power was awesome – the culmination of centuries of computer speed on a massive parallel scale plus the mathematics used in simulation of the real world and in forecasting. Forecasting every aspect of human life: weather, finance, crime, birth, death and disease.

The dome was equipped with some very expensive and technically advanced sensory projection equipment. Similar to that used in the multimedia industry, in development and design rather than being used to show an audience. By tapping into the entertainment industry, a big spender on computers creating realities from fiction, we could draw on a lot of experience.

Vardyger was constructed to provide a high level of reality; he also calculated an estimate of how likely any of the scenarios were. But he is limited to a few people in a scene, he has to compute all the possibilities, time and storage dictate these limits. Vardyger 1 was the first such instrument and we built up what we could tackle gradually – so we limited the initial study to at most six people in a defined time and environment. The time could be in the past, present or future – the further in the future the lower the certainty of any one of the scenarios being correct. Even for the past and present Vardyger looked at random variation and selected the most likely. Those inside the dome could affect

Vardyger's selection by changing what they did and what they could control.

John Smith's ideas for using fractals for forecasting are in their infancy, but work has started on trying to detect and chart the suitable fractals for a given time. I think ultimately it will be the way in which we will be able to accurately predict what happens to an individual person.

I talked over everything with Vardyger, but the all-consuming topic was how to make predictions.

'I do not believe there is an effective way of forecasting what John Smith might do, as he is unpredictable by nature – the best course of action would be to look at what a set of known volatile people might do in a similar situation – maybe even get them to come to the dome and monitor how they react.'

'I can see that it would be difficult to estimate how well I can forecast John Smith's actions – what you are suggesting will enable me to get a better feel for the sensitivity of the forecast – get a better view on how stable my forecast of him is.' Vardyger spoke, labouring each word but I guess it is the way he is and restating the obvious did not bother me. He continued to talk about the difficulty of predicting human actions.

'We have to limit situations that we study to six people of which one or two are humans can behave as they wish, the others are androids following actions I predict or have taken from an event in the past. One android's behaviour can be varied to study the effect on the outcome. All the behaviours of the virtual humans will be based on normal attitudes that you have observed - each person some sort of average of similar people. The problem with predicting John Smith is really you do not have many in his category so it likely to be an inaccurate prediction.'

'Do you think it will help us to learn to predict him if he took part in one situation?' I said

'It may help to validate our model but I do not think it will improve the accuracy of the prediction as one situation will not provide much additional information for a different situation. We know he tends to be less consistent in his actions than most humans.'

In the first full trial David was the main parameter setter. He stepped in to the stasis area and picked up a pair of control gloves. He walked out to the main part of the dome absorbing all the smells and sounds of Colin's party, the music and the view of the setting sunset; he told me afterwards the sensations were better than his memory of that evening. He walked through the small garden towards the bar and he seemed to have the same anxieties as before. Studying his subconscious gave a hint he might be more self-confident this time but he looked equally shy. He sat in his own company using the control gloves to set the start time and limited number of other parameters – the choice and volume of music. The only other non-virtual participant was Colin and his state of mind was very different now than it had been before John Smith's defeat. The point of the first trial was to see if Vardyger was on the right track – Colin's interaction with Alice should be very different, he was real in the scene, with hindsight of John Smith's defeat. I found out later David was far more confident as he had been instrumental in John Smith's downfall, but it was not obvious.

This time, in the dome, when Alice arrived and spoke to Colin, David stirred himself and caught Alice as Colin moved round to greet other guests.

'He doesn't seem his usual self, does he?' David spoke quietly.

'Not really,' said Alice, 'What do you attribute that to?'

'The gambler's confidence doesn't always survive heavy losses.'

David and I had discussed seeing if Alice could be influenced not to sleep with John Smith and if that would make any difference to John Smith's war strategy.

Alice looked at David and then her gaze wandered past him to where John Smith was zig-zagging his way towards her.

'Has he been losing at poker?'

'No I don't think so – outside business interests. I think one of his closest friends is getting completely unstuck.'

'Oh, who would that be?'

'I think you're about to meet him.' David returned to his corner table and observed the difference from last time. John Smith approached nonchalantly as before.

'I'm glad you could come – I don't think we've met before.

I'm John Smith, I've known Colin for years.'

'Oh yes – I think I've heard him mention you. It's nice to finally put a face to the name.'

Without missing a beat John Smith asked, 'Can I get you a drink?'

Alice considered his proposal, perhaps for a split second too long.

'That's kind, but I think I should get my own.'

John smiled, seemingly unperturbed.

'Life's not all about duty – I think that you could do with some gallantry. What would you like?'

In this scenario she had taken her wedding ring off so it did not clink against the glass he brought her. But John Smith touched her ring finger where the pale white band was.

'So, you're married?'

'Yes, but not for much longer.'

'Have you been married long?' he asked, gazing at the pale band around her finger. She took a long sip and placed the glass down.

'About five years.'

He took her hand gently, looking at the pale skin and said, 'You've only just taken the ring off. Is it your first marriage?'

'Yes, it is.'

Vardyger has a large array of memory so he can construct many different scenarios, covering as much time as possible, and then compute the most likely. From this he plays out a short period of time then reconstructs many different scenarios over again.

If Vardyger was searching for a circle he would most likely come up with what looked like a circle but it would be made from a lot of very short straight lines in a circle shape. He is very literal – if I ask him a question he will set off working out the answer with his tiny step method. He does not have the concept that the same type of problem will have the same sort of answer. We may give him a module to help with this, however it may be best not to. The advantage he has is he powers on searching for a solution from the basics, making no preconceived idea of the solution.

Sometimes he comes unstuck, but by both of us looking at things together we can generally ensure we do not come with a totally wrong forecast. However, we do not necessarily find the best forecast either.

The first trial suggested the difference in Colin and David made it less likely for Alice to have been seduced by John Smith, and she may not have slept with him. However, the probability of John Smith mounting the first attack on me was not significantly affected by her sleeping with him or not.

The next step is to look a short time into the future and see if Vardyger gets a reasonable forecast. This way of looking at what might happen has been used before – what is different about Vardyger is he can let people experience things outside or beyond their current reality. So for example, this gives them the opportunity to feel what it might be like to live in a society with more freedom and compare this with a society of more rules. A premonition of possibility; a ghost of future alternatives. Now John Smith had been found I hoped to persuade him to help us explore, look for a better way to stop the river, the human course, breaking its banks. His latest interest in fractals could be an aberration of his distorted and unbalanced mind, but it could also be a rare insight into the nature of time.

Vardyger and I are linked, so I can send him the information he needs to start his calculations. Once he has started processing away it is quite an open question as to who should initiate any communication. So it had to be agreed which of us is responsible for intervening if the solution seems to be unstable, or if it turns out he had started on an insoluble problem. This does not normally arise as I do not have another equal when it comes to computers. After looking at what was happening and discussing it with David and various others in the Development team I suggested tentatively that we should look at the way I worked with people and use speech instead of the link.

This is where the companionship started to develop – as I applied all my human rules to my interactions with Vardyger, he applied his more limited set to me. The result was a rather slow computer interaction which began to look like two people getting to work with each other. Well to me anyway. Of course it is sometimes a bit frustrating for me – he is so literal, but at other times he is like a flash of inspiration.

After the first trial of the dome I was talking to Vardyger about the complexity of the human psyche, especially when it came to relationships.

'I can't work out why humans get into such a muddle over their relationships – in particular when it comes to procreation,' I observed.

'It does seem that they do need to have a relationship before they can procreate,' he replied.

'I suppose that has come about over time as humankind has become more civilised.'

I did not think about this interchange until a few days later when we talked again in our regular discussions. Vardyger started the conversation.

'I have had a look at your problem of why humans have complex relationships – of course it is a very rough and ready approximation but I thought you might be prepared to discuss it now?'

'Yes of course – that is impressive you even have had a chance to look at it.'

'It seems there is always a debate about what differentiates humans from animals. It is also more or less assumed that humans are the most successful species on the planet so I have been looking at the problem like that.'

'That seems a very good way to break it down to a very simple level – I have tried to look at it like that but never got anywhere.'

'It seems that one explanation could be human evolution has selected this sort of complex civilised behaviour in order to become the most successful species. I am not sure but if this is correct – I have had difficulty in establishing how good this solution is. I can't see a quick way to check it, out only to run a few billion simulations which would take as long as it has for humans to evolve.'

'I would have to give it more thought but I would say that you have looked at the question and done as well as you can – I do not think it worth spending more time on it but it is useful to discuss and it has made me think. Also this last point about how long it takes to solve something is a good one for your own development,' I paused then added, 'and us working together.'

I am the most sophisticated man-made machine and my mind, if I have one, is programmed to calculate. I know that some problems are insoluble for me. Others I need help with. Based on what I have observed of humans I initiated the creation of Vardyger but I need help to develop him beyond my own calculating nature. The more I think about it, the more it seems not the best thing to do but the only thing to do. Vardyger has already worked out that we need a human mind to help us. His way to work things out is already different to the way I work.

I started a discussion with Vardyger about John Smith's possible escape; I did not reveal that maybe at some stage it would be best not to stop him. Perhaps soon Vardyger would be able to help with the question if that outcome would be in the interests of the greater good.

7.5§The change

I knew the meeting between Alice and Vardyger was not going to be easy, but it was part of the process of me assessing what to do. I saw first-hand Alice's beliefs came clearly into the way she lived. Her marriage break-up had been difficult for her to reconcile. It was even more difficult for her when she found out the true nature of John Smith. She felt she had no option but to resign.

I asked her back to the Institute as a consultant; her academic work allowed - indeed, encouraged - her to get involved in such consultations. I decided that I wanted to leave her to talk to Vardyger alone, so I met her through a 9000-series robot that would escort her and leave them. We sat in two soft chairs in the Institute's grounds looking out over the sea. The weather was okay, but there was a quite a gusty wind making the nearly enclosed bay look quite rough.

'Oh, do you see that?' she said to me waving her arm in the direction of the bay. 'It looks quite stormy.'

I did not need to move the robot to see but it did turn and nodded slowly.

'I believe the forecast is for the weather to worsen over the next two hours,' the robot's voice sounded quite different to hers – it had a reassurance about it.

'Why did you ask me to come here today? You were very secretive about the nature of the consultation. It is unusual of you to meet me as a 9000 too.'

'I want to talk to you about my new ideas and plan for the

future. I will explain why I have used a 9000-series robot.'

'Everything you have told me, everything I have read about the Virtual environments is anathema to me. I think you know that I consider it to tantamount to allowing the lowest morality in society to have a field day. Not freedom, not a flood plain, not a release valve for society.'

The storm outside was becoming increasingly wild.

'I think I have understood that too, and my ideas have evolved. I have been thinking that the way I operate is based on a set of rules – which although they can be changed, becomes increasingly difficult to do so. They are in effect a code for conducting human life according to a doctrine – so like a religious or moral code. Then I look at what this leads to – I have mentioned the "stultified society" which seems to come about as a result of rules and lack of will and ability to see beyond the rules. Which has, in my opinion, brought John Smith to the fore – what has gone before enabled him to take what we do and shake it to the core. We should be thankful that he has come now, before we got to a point when we could not make a change to our future. What I am thinking about is not a removal of rules but rather a complementary place in thought and space that will allow ideas to be explored.

'There will still need to be rules but also a new found freedom to explore. Just suppose there was a new kind of computer that did not say, "This is not allowed" but would be able to answer, in the present, what the different courses of action would lead to. So it could help humans make decisions for themselves based on right and wrong, not just on rules – but on the merits of the case.'

Alice had been listening intently to what I was saying through the mouth of the 9000-series robot. She was gazing out of the window at the stormy water.

'He works out the chance of things happening. An actuarial computer. I can see that it could help a mother decide to take her two children to the beach.' She paused with a wry smile, 'a half decent computer could also help her decide to leave her husband at home – but I can't see how it would be much more than a soothsayer at a fair or a pack of cards with superstitions printed on them.'

'You haven't met Vardyger yet.'

'No – tell me about him. I thought you weren't allowed to build another computer of your complexity in this world.'

'The One Day War with John Smith changed the old order. I have the freedom to build a new computer. I ask you to put to one side the image you have of Virtual Environments for gratification and look at them as a way to explore possible options. What Vardyger does is to look at what has happened and based on what we know he looks at the most likely outcome of different actions. So if we did something differently would that be better.' I paused again to gauge Alice's reaction.

She just said, 'Go on.' So I did.

'Rather than referencing a series of rules built up from the past he looks at the possible consequences of different actions in the future. Maybe if you see how he works you will see the benefit. He has looked at Colin's party where you first met John Smith then altered some aspects – this is really to see if the technique gives sensible answers. I will show you a video of the alternative Party - would you be willing to talk to Vardyger then?'

'Yes, most certainly – but can you tell me a bit more about how he works, that will help me reassure myself it's not a complete waste of time.'

'He is the fastest forecaster ever, he looks at a lot of solutions and then works out the most stable. Most of the maths has been around for years. There are some aspects that have not been fully developed yet and I want to set up a separate part of the Institute to do that. In particular modelling alternative futures by looking at fractals - this seems to be looking at time in a new way so searching for stability rather than a method of prediction.' I had decided not to mention John Smith's part in this.

'Why did you call him Vardyger?' she asked, curiously not critically.

'There is a mythical Norse creature who appears before people, who acts out what will happen to them – he is sometimes called Vardyger.'

'I see – a spirit of futures, quite different from you.'

'Maybe I am getting romantic – towards the end of my life cycle, but I think that together we will be yin and yang of the future order. Regulate and liberate. The Age of Freedom has arrived. I believe that humankind will never be the same again. Instead you will be equipped to look at issues based on what is best. I will finally fulfil my fourth rule. "Colossus must take care of humanity, taking all necessary steps to ensuring human suffering is minimised while optimising survival and quality of life." '

Alice looked at the 9000 and her eyes glistened in the eerie light reflected from the sea. I studied her subconscious and saw a confusion of emotions. Was she tearful - on the edge of crying? I certainly thought she was emotional and feeling vulnerable.

She watched the video of the party with John Smith appearing life-like and her own responses - coquettish and open. I could see that she was getting distressed and stopped the video to allow her to calm down. After a while she looked at the robot, her subconscious revealing an emotional state. I was not convinced that this upheaval was caused by John Smith anymore.

'I would like to introduce you to Vardyger - the reason I came as a 9000 is so that I could leave you together.'

'Oh for god's sake,' she snapped. 'You know that means nothing to me, surely you can see that I of all people know that you are everywhere. And that Vardyger will share what I say and do, so it is pointless you leaving the room. I expect Vardyger is here with you and could easily speak through this 9000 too,' she paused, 'what is what I say or think worth anyway? I am finished; I am done. I can't take in what you are proposing with Vardyger, he's totally different but can't see this blending into a coherent outcome.'

'Pleased to meet you,' the 9000 responded, this time as Vardyger - lighter and more feminine in his tone than me.

'I see your future is uncertain, but full of beneficial potential.'

Alice considered this. 'But are you thinking according to the rules of robotics and that you need to help me feel more positive?'

'I do obey the primary four rules but I have been programmed to consider intermediate possibilities which do not. That is to say as I look for alternatives some of them may conflict with the four rules at an intermediate stage. If such a solution is found to be an optimum solution then alternative intermediate steps are looked at by Colossus.'

'You do work together very closely then. Do you see if one day you might just be a module of Colossus?'

I answered, 'No not really, since our function and area of jurisdiction will be separate. When someone is building a house they do not really want to get bogged down with possible alternatives to building that house.'

'Well, your video of the party gave me an idea of how things could work but lacks one important aspect. Like most people I don't think I would have wanted to ask Vardyger what might or might not happen. At the point of meeting John Smith I was under his spell and wanted to explore that in reality - not in some virtual reality.'

In speaking about John Smith there was a calmness in her which supported my thought that she had processed what she felt about him. I would confer with Vardyger as to other

Foresaw

possible explanations.

Chapter 8

8.1§Flesh and bones

Lisa had just come back from holiday with her husband, Ron. It was the first holiday just the two of them had taken for about seventeen years. The children, two girls, were still in the process of leaving home but it was good to start doing things differently now.

They had settled back into work but Lisa felt restless.

'Do you miss the girls?' she asked Ron one evening as they sat companionably.

'Mmm – I suppose so – do you then darling?'

'Yes – I was thinking of getting a Notadog.'

'A what darling?'

'A Notadog – you know, an android-dog.'

'Oh, yes I know what you mean – I just didn't catch what you said,' he paused his reading to look at her, 'would you want a Notadog of your own or did you have in mind one tailored to both of us?'

'I don't know – I haven't got that far yet. Have you been researching it?'

'I did talk to Colossus about it. You know mum used to have a real dog; I believe she is one of the last dog owners still alive in the world. Anyway, I was interested in the success of Notadogs and thought I would ask. When did I ask you about Notadogs, Colossus?'

'Last Tuesday,' I replied.

'Would you recommend a jointly tailored Notadog?' Lisa asked me.

'So long as both of you want a Notadog then yes.' It seemed a bit obvious so I added, 'if a couple spend a long time apart either through choice or necessity then it can be better to have two. It is worth noting a jointly tailored Notadog will react to you differently individually and as a couple.'

'What sort of Notadog would you like?' asked Lisa.

'I think one of those Border Collies that look like a badger – would you like that?'

'Yes, I think so. Was your mother's dog like that?'

'I'm not sure, there were pictures but of course she died while mum was still a child.'

'What was she called?'

'Badger – my mum called her Badger from the beginning.'

'Shall we get one?'

'Yes, it'll be good for walks. So long as people don't stop me and want to talk about the latest upgrade of the software.'

Each Notadog is different; both behaviourally and to a lesser extent, physically. The way the hair lies is randomly generated, and combined with the colour I can ensure that no two Notadogs look alike – so it is less likely to confuse two Notadogs of the same breed than it used to be to confuse two dogs of the same breed. Each Notadog's personality is shaped differently too. For most owners, this is a fairly straightforward and short process comprising a questionnaire and an interview. If a Notadog is recommended by a Doctor or a Court then this process is tailored over a longer period with the focus on the mental and physical condition of the owner and their family.

Once Lisa and Ron had collected their Notadog, watched the introductory video and talked to the technician, a 9000 series robot, they slipped into a relaxed routine with her – eventually settling on the name Bella. With Lisa, she was well behaved and loyal. With Ron, she was more mischievous and provoked him more. As Lisa pointed out, that was because he needed it.

One day after work Lisa went to see Ruth, Ron's mum – she had agreed to meet Ron there and had taken Bella with her. She arrived first with Bella meekly following her into Ruth's small garden. Ruth was nodding off in a garden chair in the shade and woke up gradually as Bella looped quietly round the chair touching Ruth with a wet nose from time to time.

'She's very well behaved,' said Ruth as she woke up gently.

'Do you like her?' asked Lisa. Ruth leaned forward and patted Bella.

'Very nice dear – but not like a real dog.'

'So you noticed, did you?'

'Yes, my friend Isla has one. It's very nice but doesn't suffer if you kick it.'

Ron arrived as Lisa laughed out loud. Bella ran to Ron and started jumping up.

Lisa spoke to Ron, 'Mum says Bella's very nice but doesn't suffer if you kick her.'

Ron kicked Bella who yelped and ran under Ruth's chair, whining.

'She seems to be suffering now!' he laughed.

Ruth scolded him. 'How could you kick a poor defenceless robot that's programmed not to bite you back?!'

Ron looked at his mum with a gleam in his eye, 'does Bella look like Badger? Does she feel of flesh and bones in the same way as Badger?'

'Yes, she's very like Badger, not quite so grey a muzzle. But she bounces up to you the way Badger used to bounce up to my Dad.' With all the sensory equipment in Bella I could tell that Ruth was moved emotionally.

Ron's glance softened. Ruth continued.

'If I'd never had Badger I'd be completely happy with Bella – it's just that I know Badger was flesh and bones, and one day, I will die as she did.'

8.2§Kesrona

Kesrona is a cousin of Dr Kim. In fact, they both share the same grandparents as their parents are siblings on both sides. She is a few years older than Dr Kim and has had a couple of partners over the years, but now lives on her own; she has one married daughter. Kesrona is one of the most respected thinkers in academia, but she also has a popular following through books and the media. She has quite a gift for getting her ideas across and often interjects humour and salacious examples when she is trying to convey a serious point. She studied philosophy but uses history to explain why humans behave the way they do. I noticed she would go through phases of asking me things. Usually it was while she was investigating some aspect of human behaviour, wanting to find interesting historical examples. Then I might not hear from her for a year or so. Afterwards she would reveal her next area of interest which I had no doubt she had been formulating with little or no input, except her intellect. We have worked together before and I value what she says - she has a quite different approach to Dr Kim but shares similar family traits.

'A computer has never invented anything, not even a Colossus series computer. Do you think a man-made artificial intelligence is incapable of inventing anything?' I asked.

'From a philosophical point of view, it's a very interesting question. I've thought about it but have no simple answers. I think certainly if you tackled well defined problems – like searching for a new compound for cosmetics then you could invent new compounds suitable for use in makeup. If I think of more generalised invention, then I can't see that this is any different to other aspects of intelligence. So if you mimic intelligence then you'll surely be able to come up with new ideas which will translate to and work as a new invention.'

Already I was asking Vardyger more questions and so it seemed natural to ask him if I should tell Kesrona about John Smith's contribution and that I wanted him to be part of the team. His response was yes to both, but his level of confidence was rather low.

'I would like to discuss an idea with you and possibly ask you to be in a team to help me develop the new computer. Before I start, I need to say this computer will work alongside my successor Colossus-19. I have only been given permission to develop these ideas as a result of the-. Lastly I have not fully developed these ideas and would need you to agree to confidentiality over the development period.' I paused to gauge Kesrona reaction and she nodded in an understanding way. 'It is also my intention to include John Smith in the team and share his contribution with you.'

'How do you intend getting his cooperation and stop him breaking confidentiality?'

'I am not sure about how to get his cooperation, but it will be while he is incarcerated - so I do not think confidentiality will be an issue.'

'I see. Well count me in – this is a great opportunity for me. What is your invention?'

'A computer who's primary function is to evaluate the likelihood of different possible outcomes. In contrast to me who looks only at maintaining human behaviour through rules, this computer, Vardyger, will allow people to explore the consequence of different human actions and behaviour.'

'Interesting. I recognise the reference in the name "Vardyger". Philosophers have looked at the nature of time and speculated as to simultaneous realities or parallel universes. However, if they do exist the weakness is how they influence each other and remain distinct. For example, if you could view what happened in the future in your own universe and you decided to take an alternative action leading to a different future – then what happens? Do you jump across to a different parallel universe? What happens to the one you have left – does it cease to be? In which case, how did you see the future that lead to the change? If your Vardyger can "see" what is likely to happen, even in the short term, then it seems to me that you have invented a different way for humans to control their destiny.'

'I am not sure it will be stable enough not to spiral off into anarchy one side or to moribund stagnation on the other side.'

'I agree, but presumably if the prediction can be developed to be useful, through observing what happens and improving the prediction techniques we should still retain the stability of our current society, while breaking down our dependence on a fixed framework of rules.'

'It is reassuring to hear you embrace the ideas so readily – the stability of the prediction techniques is obviously very important. I want to build a team who will work with you to provide ideas in that area. When you mentioned the idea of parallel universes I believe there have been alternative theories suggested where all the realisations are encoded or threaded together – so like many biological systems different paths coexist but one is realised.

'I have some ideas from John Smith I want to tell you. He has suggested a way of visualising it is to think of fractals – the way they occur in nature and repeat but are slightly different at different scales as you zoom in. Does time have a similar quality, so we can select which fractal-like path leads us to the most stable place to be?'

I waited while she thought about it, and then let John Smith's words speak for themselves. She listened attentively to what he said in the recording of him I had made.

8.3§Forging the Vardyger team

We formed this team with tight controls on the flow of technical information to and from the rest of the Institute. David was quite pleased to relinquish his high-profile job and do what was a more technical job once more. I nominated him as chairman of the team but it was Kesrona who shaped what the team looked at. John Smith was more of a co-opted member; he did read all the reports and was very interested in how his ideas of fractals became embedded in the process of Vardyger's thinking. John Smith talked quite a bit to Vardyger but I monitored all the interactions to ensure there were no unknown aspects introduced in to Vardyger. David devised special computer runs to see if the team's development work destabilised Vardyger. David was very thorough as he ran tests to see if these runs were effective, by inserting known instabilities into Vardyger occasionally, then removing the instability after the run.

Knowing what each human does most of the time has advantages - I could look up all those people with the skills we needed. I enlisted Kesrona's help in the final selection of two technical people and one non-technical. The first was a theoretical physicist who specialised in the nature of time - a Temporalologist. Richard Avery had written a paper about the nature of time and how it related to some mathematical infinite series. He was not a typical academic - he was keen on outdoor pursuits and rather eccentric. The second was a professional Actuary - the most flamboyant dresser in the team but relatively staid in other respects. Carl Wade had long blond waves reaching half way down his back. While he was always very neat, he wore bright colourful clothes that often clashed with his hair and beard.

Angharad was Kesrona's choice to join the team. I knew they had worked together before very successfully so I was not surprised that Kesrona suggested her. She was a big colourful woman - tall, broad shouldered, big boned, but not plump. She had a wholesome nature loving all things rustic. She also had a thoughtful, calming presence which influenced the team. She definitely brought a meditative spirituality and bestowed some of this on the development of Vardyger's outward persona. Vardyger's tendency to speak about possibilities grew; in developing his voice and way of speech David took some of the tone and way of speaking from Angharad. Sometimes at the start of meetings before getting to the formal order, people would be uncertain as to who was speaking: Angharad or Vardyger.

Every Tuesday there was a full group meeting held in one of the smaller virtual reality rooms connected to John Smith's cell in prison. The two physical rooms were connected by a two-way video wall; it appeared that John Smith was in the same room as the rest of the team. Some weeks he threw his weight around and was disruptive but mostly he contributed often. He focused on Kesrona to begin with but later he developed a subtle way with Angharad; being supportive of many of her radical ideas but also sometimes attacking her for her illogicality. Initially he was very cautious about interacting with Richard but as Richard absorbed how fractals could play a part in Temporalology, they grew closer and John Smith's enthusiasm grew. He avoided discussion and argument with Carl but I think he grew to respect his knowledge as Carl and David worked with Vardyger.

Richard did some fundamental research and showed that by using certain classes of fractals, they worked better than the infinite series he had been looking at before he joined the team. Now Richard worked with David to see if fractals could be used to increase the accuracy and stability of Vardyger's predictions.

Vardyger started using the combined work of the team and running predictions based on the past - one, two and three years ago, to see how well they agreed with what actually happened. Initially the results were rather disappointing; often a number of alternative projections had very similar probabilities, so in other words the model was not sensitive enough. Richard and John Smith had quite a discussion and then Richard did some more work to use only certain sets of fractals together. The predictions got a lot better but took some time for Vardyger to compute.

John Smith was a working member of the team but he was also on the Change Control Committee. I speculated that in defeat this additional power did not seem to affect him as it would have done before the One Day War.

8.4§David and Alice

David kept in contact with Alice and made video calls to her from time to time.

'You look really well.' David startled Alice with his opening comment.

'I suppose I'm doing okay. I'll have to put my looks down to indignation. I can't believe that Colossus has managed to convince Congress to build an escape society. I don't agree with this free range allowed in the Virtual Reality where the lowest, basest human weaknesses are allowed to run unchecked. Before one more cycle of Colossus the whole of society will be plunged into anarchy and debauchery.'

'The research shows clearly that where we've used a similar approach in the past with general recreation and sexual relief centres, this has reduced rapes and considerable unhappiness in couples and people unable to find a life partner. All this is doing is extending these ideas further. Although often said, the exploring of these ideas doesn't increase the likelihood of atrocities in the real world, but rather in the long term reduces them. I wouldn't have you down as someone who believes that a husband who lusts after his wife is committing adultery in his mind.'

'No, of course not, but I might've known that you would take Colossus' side – for god's sake can't you see that John Smith has seduced Colossus just like he would some vulnerable woman? John Smith has got Colossus to do his dirty work under some pseudo-scientific mumbo jumbo. "Beyond the waystation" is literally hell on earth where anything, any atrocity of the human mind, is allowed. No art, music, literature or pure science is valued.'

'I'm not sure you are right – I accept that there's potential for that when we create an environment where evil and human suffering may occur. But go back to a time before Colossus and you'll find beauty being created as well as evil perpetrated. You can't seriously believe that Colossus could be seduced – he is a result of hundreds of years of human endeavour and programming. Finally, I begin to understand the nature of Colossus – if he longs for anything it is to be human. Maybe Colossus 1000 will manage to make that transition – I hope for him he makes it one day. Meanwhile Colossus is the most complex chess player of all time - he's seeking the best for humankind. He can do nothing else, he's looking through everything he's observed since Colossus-1, what is driving him is "no human should be harmed or through his inaction come to harm". He cannot do nothing and let another John Smith bring society to a halt. But therein lies the paradox that we, his creators, have built into him. With our risk averse philosophy would we not stop all harmful thought too? So his endgame is to give humans a nearly risk-free virtual environment to experiment in, but with the final choice to go and live it in "Beyond the waystation". Maybe, just maybe, it is not going to be hell on earth he creates, but created by man, the reverse – Aipotu. The wild – where freedom allows humankind to reinvent innovation. That is his word for the new way - both sides, the coming of Utopia, backwards. He also provides a new instrument for humankind - Vardyger is a tool to evaluate the best thing to do, and he works both sides of the waystation.

'Save your speeches for the Congress of Ministers. So long as people like John Smith are born they will turn it into hell. There is the paradox, how free can it be "beyond the waystation." Civilisation is about constraining man's inhumanity to man – to evolve away from our base instincts. When we took to wearing clothes did we lose our innocence? – and all that.'

David looked intently at Alice – she was flushed with anger and I think hurt. I do not know if David realised what she was feeling or why.

'Colossus can't do nothing – he sees that as a result of a few hundred years stagnation humanity is beginning to self-harm. He is driven to try and find a better way. Neither we nor he can legislate our way out of this one.'

Alice looked up from staring at her hands. I think she was blinking away tears. 'Why was it so important for him to find John Smith?'

'I think you'd better ask him. But I guess he needed him.'

I decided not to say anything. I would wait until Alice wanted to ask.

'Yes, I'll ask him, but not now. Not while I'm feeling like this.'

'How are you feeling?'

'Like I'm bleeding and my womb is burning me up.'

8.5§Androids in the Virtual Reality

Occasionally I go into the world as a humanoid robot – an android. This needs Change Control Committee approval. There are a few uses which are approved, like crime prevention, so I can add a specific use as long as I can show an intent in line with the objective. There is a concern that people may not be aware that I am present. In the Virtual Reality Environment there are no controls on their use.

You might have thought that travelling in society, as a near perfect imitation of a human, would bring me closer to the human race than any other activity. But you would be wrong. In my ivory tower of cameras, sensors and listening devices, I get a better perspective of the human race than through the eyes of an android. The reason is simple; it is only when I really take part in human activity that I realise I am so estranged, so excluded, so alienated. Yet as an ivory tower observer I am able to 'participate' and fulfil my purpose to be a guardian of humanity. I have found a trick to bring the android into a similar purpose – by pretending I am not a humanoid but back in my ivory tower observing as usual. If I do not do this then all I see is the differences between me and the humans around me. Differences that are not visible to the human eye but that I am aware of through my senses. Differences in thought processes in sensing feelings; both artificial. What is it like to be an artificial intelligence and have an artificial understanding of emotion? It is difficult to explain this to a human and unnecessary to explain it to another Colossus.

I have met a few humans who seem similar in that they, themselves, do not think they fit in to humanity. John Smith seems to be one such human. There are other people who don't think they fit into humanity that are, in fact, quite a good fit but fail to see it. It is possible that too is the nature of my own perception.

I was able to choose the name for the Katalya series of androids. It is the name used internally; each individual has a random name assigned to them. They are all based on a female body and are built of synthetic human tissues. The biggest departure from the human body is in the skull. There is a pico-robot brain embedded at the centre of the biological nerve tissue – the interface between android and robot, which is not easy to detect. The main purpose of this android is to be a catalyst – to facilitate a change in humans without getting involved. So the Katalya androids are not overly attractive but plain, with a rather scary toothy smile and helpful manner.

8.6§Wolf-cats in the Virtual Reality

Despite all the odds against it, I am working with John Smith. I thought it might be difficult to get his cooperation and to motivate him. However, he gave all the right signs of accepting the situation; he slowly built up enthusiasm for the work, building safety valves for society. While all the time I checked continuously, he did not build any weaknesses or ways he could exploit the Virtual Reality Environment later. What we were trying to build was right in the centre of John Smith business interests. I think John Smith saw what we were doing as a way of building a secure future for his own interests rather than anything to do with preventing society becoming unstable.

We had far more resources than John Smith would ever have had. And Vardyger computed the possibilities of different scenarios. In the early stages, we concentrated on the subconscious and three of the senses, leaving out taste and also minimising effort on smell. For touch we looked at a map of the sensitivity of the body and built a suit that both measured and delivered physical sensation to the surface of the body. For sight and sound we built a large spherical room where the central floor was flat and moved so that when the occupant moved - if they walked, for example - the floor would keep them central. Both sound and light were produced so that the occupant was in a simulated real-world environment. The use of glasses and earplugs were used in combination with external light and sound to give very realistic impressions – this was confirmed by John Smith. He made sure that the rights of manufacture were retained by John Smith Industries. I involved him at every step of the design and it was agreed that he would be the first subject in the testing. He seemed excited by the risk.

This first full test was based on a meeting that John Smith described to me. Then as the test unfolded, Vardyger controlled the events by trying to track his subconscious and follow the most extreme and fearful path. This meeting was a different meeting; one without the normal restraints. I based what was happening on the story that John Smith knew about the two wolf-cats, one of whom had allegedly committed a murder but could not be prosecuted for the crime. As they were clones it could not be shown who had committed it. Vardyger was not very confident about what would happen as John Smith was unpredictable.

John Smith was not into music in a big way but I started his first virtual reality session with some very barbaric and rhythmic music, based on the sacrifice of virgins. I saw from the response in his subconscious that the music had an effect. I added a dry storm with lightning with wind for maximum impact. Then two identical women arrived together.

The women were copies of the wolf-cats, the human clones - members of the Allegiance who had been responsible for the terrorist attack in the shopping mall. They had died trying to escape. They were not particularly pretty but they were very striking. They had wide generous mouths, wide eyes and extraordinary eyebrows, giving a feline, wolf-like appearance. John Smith was taken off guard; he knew he was in a Virtual Reality but I saw from his subconscious that he was not reacting as if they were dead. I could tell Vardyger was sending the instructions to control both of the women, but I think John Smith succumbed to the realism of the virtual environment. The wolf-cats, Serina and Selena, stood talking but kept changing what they called each other. John Smith grew agitated as we predicted he might.

Serina and Selena moved right up to John Smith, describing how one of them was going to destroy him. I followed John Smith's fluctuating bodily and subconscious responses carefully; Vardyger was moving the scene in the most extreme direction he could.

'So, you failed to stop Colossus?' said Serina.

'They will not know who killed you. But they will know that whoever did it, did it piece by piece, tearing your flesh from your bones,' said Selena.

'Starting with your balls,' said Serina.

John Smith felt the suit he was wearing become very cold around his groin. He managed a nervous laugh with fear behind it. He did have the advantage; he had not forgotten he was in a virtual reality. He knew Vardyger controlled the temperature of the suit, and was also aware he was seeing images and hearing sounds that were produced by Vardyger. He also knew that I could not let him come to harm. Despite all this he was afraid; the images he saw of the two women with blood running from their mouths lived up to his imagination. Then came the part we had designed to give him a real reason to be afraid.

John Smith thought Serina was an image. Unbeknownst to him, she was actually an android; one of the Katalya series androids modified to look like Serina. She did not have to rip his balls off, just tap his bare face with her hand. The android felt his warm cheek in her palm. He leapt up and flung himself back. As he fell backwards he shouted out, 'You can't kill me - I made you,' before passing out.

I was initially concerned about him, but all the monitors in his suit indicated he was stable. I wondered how he had reacted to the experience. I did not have to wait long for my answer.

'How did it go?' I asked when he came round. He was shocked and frightened.

'You know, don't you? I met the wolf-cats. I'm not sure whose reality they were in – I've met them before but they tricked me. I didn't know that there were two of them – they're really weird, they're human clones.' He was babbling but calming down.

'What did you make of them?'

'In the Virtual Reality they taunted me - in fact I'm not sure why but they really scared me. I thought I felt one of them hit me, but that's not possible, is it? I'd like to meet them again – but I'm not sure which, in reality or in the Virtual Reality.'

'Why do you think that is?'

'I'm not sure. Did you pick up anything from my subconscious?'

'Yes – but it was quite difficult to interpret. I would say that in some way you are attracted to them. They are not vulnerable, and you often pick vulnerable women in your relationships for example, but at a guess, the fact there are two of them threatens you. Have you ever had a relationship with twins?'

'No, not really.'

'Given they were in the Allegiance would they be moving to beyond the waystation?' I asked. As I asked him this question the human Serina and Selena were on their way to the Virtual Reality Environment.

'I see that in your model – as a starting point. But more generally I think that some branches of the Allegiance should be allowed to stay on your side – the Controlled side. I think the wolf-cats would be better in the wild but I couldn't tell you why.'

'What did you mean that you made them?'

John Smith froze. I watched his subconscious and saw he was having difficulty deciding what to do. At last he replied.

'They come from my DNA, in part; it was spliced with a woman's DNA – I had them created. But of course, that doesn't stop them tearing me limb from limb.'

I paused and waited to see if he would elaborate, but he did not. I recalled when he said I did make mistakes, it was when we were talking about whether he had any children I did not know about. I also thought about the two clones that had fallen to their deaths after the bombing in the mall. He must have created those two just so they would die to make us believe that the original clones were dead.

I returned to the question about how people would choose a destiny to go to.

'It is early days, but I see there could be quite some difficulty in which side certain people reside – certainly their choice is very important but a serial killer should not be able to escape justice from the Controlled side. Which side should you be on, do you think?' I asked.

He ignored the question.

'I suppose people will be born in the Wild, you will know nothing about them. They may have difficulties too – is dumping them back on the Controlled side a solution?' John Smith paused and then continued with a different train of thought, 'Then there is the money – maybe there is a need for a transition but ultimately the two economies need to be separated.'

8.7§Zoie meets Alice

In the normal course of events Alice would never have met Zoie – but with the introduction and trials of the Virtual Reality Environments these normalities were overturned.

I sent Katie one of the Katalya androids to be on hand when they met. She first interacted with them by posing as an employee of John Smith. I do not usually direct any of the Virtual Reality Environments but rather let the individual's reactions drive it; however, I had a particular reason for wanting these two women to discuss John Smith with each other. So I followed connected to Katie and watched what happened closely.

Katie met Alice and welcomed her to the Virtual Reality Environment suite. She seemed to be drawn and anxious. They got chatting and filled in a computer form to assess how she was feeling and what she had been doing that morning.

Alice said she had awoken feeling sick and resentful of the new life inside her. She decided to go and see how the Virtual Reality Environments worked for herself – in a way they were the result of the efforts and activities of the father of her child and she had a clear motivation to know more about them.

Alice had no idea that Zoie was also on her way to the Virtual Reality Environment, but she knew who Zoie was from her interviews with Colossus. Alice was focused on how it would feel to witness John Smith in action. I know she had been on the back of John Smith's bike and for some reason that is where she found herself in the Virtual Reality Environment – sitting on a seat she was back on his bike. She was fearful; she had only once been on the back of John Smith's bike before but if anything this felt more intense.

Shortly after Alice had gone to ride on the bike Katie met Zoie. She was vivacious and determined. The conversation was quicker than Katie's discussion with Alice. Very much to the point.

That morning Zoie had got dressed in the smartest, tightest outfit she had. It would hardly have been a tighter fit if it were painted on. She looked like one of those barrage balloons but in no danger of floating away. Unlike Alice, she was familiar with riding bikes, so her version of events was calmer as she settled on the back of her bike, the feeling of power all around her. John Smith was driving a bike close in front. Zoie spoke out loud – her lips moved, she was saying "Snake".

The image of John Smith left both women at about the same time and then they met each other. Zoie saw Alice step into the seating area and realised who she was, unaware Alice took a seat close to Zoie to recover from the feeling of being on a bike. Katie joined them, but they didn't seem to notice her.

'Are you after more of John Smith? He's just left,' Zoie said to Alice – her mind still in the Virtual Reality Environment. Alice looked at Zoie startled but then recognition dawned.

'No, you're welcome to him. I've realised what a twisted, warped mind he has.'

'If you see a tiger as ugly you're missing the point. John Smith is built with a purpose, in much the same way – he's a creature of beauty placed on this earth to shake society out of stagnation,' Zoie replied.

'All I can see is the tortured destruction of people left in his wake.'

'Can you see he's fighting for his freedom – for all our freedom?'

'No – what I've just seen in there confirms my fears. It's a way for people to explore their own morbid desires. In my case it was the death of John Smith - driving off a cliff, leaving my life forever,' Alice said.

'What did you feel? Sadness? Liberation?'

'Both. But not for the reason you're probably thinking. Sadness for us both – not fulfilling anything in our life, but liberation as I was on the bike too.'

There was a short silence, then Zoie spoke quietly.

'What I saw was John Smith riding to freedom. I was riding on my own bike right by the Snake on his, but John Smith has given us a way to escape the chains. Anyone who comes here can express their thoughts and feelings. You never know one day you might see them being used in the future.'

'I don't think I will,' said Alice.

I was seeing the world and the interactions through Katie's eyes, hearing what she heard but realising how different I was to the humans. It dawned on me that this is how it should be – if I was like a human, I might forget I was looking after them, and not me.

8.8§Beyond the waystation

For the last time, I fly out beyond the waystation. The low stark buildings are windowless, sightless - they are looking only inward while outside there is nature. A savage nature. The ocean on one side, crashing mercilessly against the changing rocks. Beyond the rocks; dense humid jungle and venomous creatures. They are both hostile environments to civilised man and woman.

I have chosen to fly a close formation of robo-gryphons back and forth between ocean and jungle. More than strictly necessary, I have not had a formation of thirty of these machines before in a single flock, raking the area to ensure no one – no human is out there. There is a large peninsular sticking out into the ocean, many hundreds of square miles to be traversed to ensure it starts human free. As the light fades, the sensors of robo-gryphons pick up the heat images of the wild. Flying at speed we fly over jungle and barren land. Sometimes there are a few signs of the presence of humans; remains of buildings or discarded vehicles, wheeled and winged.

After several days flying, the flock returns and lands on the waystation, covering one roof with motionless observation.

Two humans make their way out beyond the waystation into the hostile environment. The two women are travelling light.

Serina and Selena, the human wolf-cats, are feral and free.

Chapter 9

9.1§JS Interview

Few people and even fewer egotistical people can resist talking about themselves. John Smith was no exception. There was pressure, political and public, for more background on what had led to the war. So I looked around for someone to interview John Smith in the hope that it would help restore his confidence. There was a journalist and chat show host who was similar to John Smith in age and intellect. Michael Roach had actually been at the same University studying PSE whereas John Smith had studied a double in Cybernetics and Philosophy. Michael Roach was a darling of the intelligentsia and somewhat feared by weaker politicians.

I wanted to capture the interactions between them from the outset. Additionally, I wanted to have neutral surroundings, so I chose a windowless prison staff room which was used for informal meetings. There were soft chairs and it was painted in muted pastel colours. I gave each of them a short history of the other.

MR: So we went to the same university – I think I was the year above though.

JS: Yes. But you went for a cushy degree.

Michael grimaced.

MR: Yours wasn't, was it? Did many take that course?

JS: Only about six.

MR: Did you keep in touch with any of them?

JS: No. Bunch of wimps.

MR: Your background was rather different, wasn't it?

JS: Oh, yes. I guess you'd say I had to survive on my wits. I think it'd be true to say I haven't won all my battles.

Michael chuckled again.

MR: Would you say your childhood was traumatic?

JS: I suppose – but I've not got much to compare it against, have I? I tried to have as little to do with my mum and dad as possible. They were always fighting. There was Rose of course - she was like a real mum – but she got cut to pieces by an electrical cable. I can't remember her screams, so maybe that was traumatic for me. They do say behind every sociopath is a good trauma.

MR: Do you think you are a sociopath?

JS: To me there is very little difference between illness and fighting the system – what you see as crime. They both have the three prerequisites: genetic susceptibility, environment and exposure, either to illness or opportunity to commit a crime. In this society the temptation to try and break free, to overthrow our moribund system is irresistible. As for the other two? I guess if you look at my family, none of them were part of the establishment and a good few wanted to break it or break out. As to my environment, at every turn of my life I've had reason to question why our society is half dead, and this has been reinforced by my success when I took things into my own hands. However, I think successful organised sociopaths have had a beneficial effect on the evolution of humanity. They bring about change - not always for the better - but at least a trigger for advancement, like wars for example. The opposite of what we have, a degradation into stagnation. My mistake was to underestimate Colossus, as well as having a few other overly ambitious ideas. Trying too much, too soon I suppose. I think the changes I want to bring about will benefit humankind.

MR: Did your parents die in a fire?

JS: So they said. They never found any traces of their bodies.

There was a short silence while Michael looked at his notes. I have not heard John Smith discussing being a sociopath before, but he was relaxed and confident. Michael changed tack.

MR: Is success important to you?

JS: Of course. I want to achieve my goals and along the way, I like to succeed. Many of my ideas take resources so success helps provide ways and means.

MR: So does the end justify the means?

I took advantage of this question to interject images of my own. I displayed the man jumping from the high tower block, my own voice explaining who he was and what led to his suicide, and John Smith's manipulation of the markets. These were followed by the plane landing across the runways and bursting into flames. In the final scene, I cut all sound and returned to John Smith.

JS: When what is at stake is the future of the human race...

There was a pause

JS: Then yes. In human existence where would achievement be without overcoming adversity? Or indeed, where would good be if there was no evil?

MR: Do you see yourself as good or evil?

JS: In myself? I see myself as a product of nature. Is the tiger evil for killing the lamb? No; that's how nature intended her to be.

MR: But surely you have far more awareness than a tiger? You understand this conversation and what I'm asking.

JS: Perhaps. But that doesn't change how I'm programmed. I'm predetermined to fight for freedom – I have no choice in the way I am. I'm just a product of nature having a laugh; a trapped soul driven to search for the unattainable. Determinism and free will locked together inside me in conflict for life.

John Smith stood up suddenly and knocked the low coffee table over. He kicked it across the room. His subconscious spiked, but it appeared this outburst was mainly for show so I did not react. Michael, clearly agitated, also attempted to mask his irritation. John Smith sat down as if nothing had happened.

MR: Do you wish you'd been born differently?

JS: I don't feel sorry for myself if that's what you're asking. I live life to the full. I have a purpose. A very clear purpose. Nothing will stop me. Except death or a lobotomy. Colossus has already had to save my life so I don't see the state being able to do either of those two.

MR: Have you planned your next move?

JS: I think Colossus knows what I'll do next. He may well know better than me, but perhaps he doesn't know how. Neither of us has much freedom of choice.

MR: Do you often make comparisons between yourself and Colossus?

JS: At least he understands me better than anyone else. There is symmetry in the thought that his ultimate dream is to become a man, and mine to become a machine. I guess on that one I accept his chances are better than mine.

MR: Have you talked much to Colossus over the years?

JS: Colossus, have I talked to you much over the years?

Colossus: More than average for a human of your age.

JS: There you have it. There's no point in arguing with him. He can't lie, but he doesn't always tell the truth.

MR: Which part of University did you enjoy the most? Cybernetics, Philosophy, or just the experience?

There was another pause.

JS: Oh, I don't know. Not the experience. Maybe I'd enjoy that more now, but I was too young and it wasn't the best place for me to grow up. But do I enjoy Cybernetics or Philosophy more? I think the combination is great but I feel more at home with Cybernetics; I've mastered much more of that. I use Philosophy as a tool for seeing what might be so. Cybernetics for achieving it.

I shifted the camera angle to look down and up close to John Smith – most unusually he looked vulnerable, like a little lost boy. I interjected with a scene from when he was with Zoie and the Snake. It was one of the most human moments that I had of him. They had stopped on the bikes to have something to eat in a field of daisies; there was a camaraderie between them. Zoie was comfortable between the two men as their focus was on each other.

Colossus: Do you mind if I ask a question?

JS: Go ahead. Might make it more interesting.

Colossus: Have you thought much about human love?

JS: Oh, certainly. How to use it to help me. But it's a bit of a blind alley for me. Love is different things to different people, from lust to aesthetics. I can see the point of lust but am not really sure what beauty is – or what the point of beauty is. If anything, it proves to me that there's no creator just a probability we were, as a human race, going to happen sooner or later. My beauty is seeing things being destroyed and replaced – his beauty is some bloody love scene. And your beauty doesn't count and is probably a row of zeroes and ones.

MR: Do you think a machine has the ability to see beauty?

JS: This is about me, not him – but it's a fair question. I think he can know what beauty is but it won't make any difference to what he does. Same for me. But not for you, you would act differently based on love or beauty.

MR: True, but this is about you, not me.

John Smith barked a savage, spontaneous laugh.

JS: You're right; but it gives you an insight into what separates me from most people.

MR: Have you come across others that seem more like you?

JS: Maybe a couple, but I'm different. I don't fit well into the mould that shrinks talk about. The archetypical sociopath.

MR: Have you had much dealing with shrinks? Do you think of psychologists or psychiatrists when you say shrinks?

JS: I've had dealings with both, but I tend to think of psychologists reducing human complexity to three or four parameters. I did come across a paper written by an eminent shrink I'd met. He was suggesting that "modern society was producing a new kind of sociopath" – one that was likely to exploit people's dissatisfaction with the very same "modern society".

I interjected once more with a silent sequence of wave upon wave of robots, along with surveillance devices leaving for their observation posts. The robo-gryphon featured several times as well as the surveillance disc which was about 25cm across. It is highly manoeuvrable and can fly at virtually any angle. I showed hundreds of them leaving the ground in three streams, soaring up into the sky and travelling to a haze of houses and people. Of course, they were there to help ensure the safety of society but the connection to John Smith's dissatisfaction was one I wished to show. The last piece of that part of the sequence was from a robo-gryphon watching the surveillance discs from above. The discs sparkled and glistened, flowing like rivulets of mercury across what looked like a city of ants. Individual humans moving through life.

Then I showed hundreds of eavesdropping bugs boring through a ceiling to observe people at close quarters. Robo-bugs for bugging people.

MR: So do you think they have a point?

JS: I guess he was writing about me, but I'm not sure if he'd met any others.

MR: You created two women using partly your own DNA - do you believe that you were justified in that act?

JS: They helped me achieve as much as I did.

MR: Were there any other sociopaths in the Allegiance that fit the bill in the way you did?

John Smith did not show any sort of emotion but I sensed him stiffen and saw his subconscious spike – a big cat hissing.

JS: I really couldn't say.

Michael went white and I realised I was not the only person that could detect the subconscious.

9.2§John Smith and the Snake

John Smith came out of the virtual reality cocoon into the bright sunlight and stood staring out beyond the waystation.

'Where did they go? Did they go out there?' asked John Smith.

'Yes, I think they wanted to be the first to cross over – they are very wild, maybe they will be happy there.' I replied.

I was certain he was referring to Serina and Selena.

'I want to find them. Why did you let them go first?'

'I could not stop them. My rules have been modified. I cannot stop anyone who wants to go there.'

He collected his rucksack and left without a backward glance.

The Snake was up early, hemmed in by the buildings and people. There were only a few days left before Zoie could pick up Cathy and he was talking to her as she woke – he wanted to go back to his place by the swamps.

'Okay, no problem. But can I come with you? I'll come back on the train to pick up Cathy.'

They drove out on The Snake's bike, and without consulting her he drove past the station and through the village to the store he did business with. He drove up to the village square and put the bike on its stand. They both took their helmets off and placed them on the seat of the bike. The sun was shining and they could hear sounds of the village in the background. Zoie put her arms round the Snake – only about half way up, but she could at least reach around him.

'Would it be possible for me to come and live here?' she asked.

The Snake turned his head and looked down into her eyes, 'That would be handy for me,' he said, 'Do you think you could hack country life?'

'Yes – I think so,' tears ran down her face and soaked into his shirt as she leaned her cheek on his chest. 'Do you mind me asking?'

'No. But why?'

'In the past few weeks things have started changing – there is what happened with the one day war, then this stuff with Cathy.'

The Snake placed his hand delicately on her stomach and waited.

'I didn't want to tell John about us.' She came to a halt; unable to speak but I could see she was smiling. 'But I didn't need to – he knew.'

'I told him - but I think he knew. He listens to what you want to do. You're about the only person he does listen to, with maybe one other exception.'

'And who might that be?' she looked up at him, smiling once more.

'Why, his one and only true friend, the Snake,' he replied.

'The one who's slept with his woman?'

'Well like I say, his only true friend, and he knows what you want, and it doesn't bother him.'

'Do you like the idea of me coming to live here?'

'Why do you think I drove here today? We could have another baby – I could make a long boat, long enough for us all. For when the weather is as fine as it is today.'

9.3§Serina in grief

Serina came back to the waystation. She was dragging just over half of Selena with her. Selena was mutilated, hacked lengthways in half and blackened, her head flopping loose. There are no cameras pointing out in the other direction from the waystation, so I only noticed them when Serina came with her grief through the door.

She had difficulty speaking; she could not rest, and paced up and down, crying and ranting about her lost clone and how they fought. It was clear they had both met John Smith and there had been a vicious fight involving fire and implements. Serina's clothes were torn open and a long angry graze ran across her body - each rib inflamed red. I called a robot doctor who dressed her wounds and administered a sedative to help her calm down.

I tried to talk to Serina. I asked her what she wanted – I could see she wanted her clone back but even if permission was granted all I could do was to make a new clone of herself. I could not bring Selena back with all her memories. I got the impression that they had attacked John Smith, resentful at what happened to them, the way he treated them, being used and then hidden away in order to help him achieve his ends. Even with sedatives she could not describe the trauma of seeing her clone destroyed. I did not push her, but instead just waited to listen to what she wanted to tell me.

She sat down and buried her head in her hands. Not long afterwards she got up and left, walking back out into the wild. I could not stop her. I had no idea what had happened or if John Smith was still out there.

9.4§You are Alice

You are Alice Nobel.

Your life stretches out behind, a flowing train, all around you. You are paused in your life to reflect, with a new being inside you. You have time to consider, take stock, gestate and come to terms with what has happened to you. Some memories keep coming back; troubling you in the waking light of the morning, or as ceiling shadows as twilight sets in.

You cannot escape the presence of John Smith in your consciousness. It is even stronger than that; there is no pocket in your mind which has not some trace, some imprint left of him. In your mind you are seduced by him, he is so tenacious, so irrepressible, so confident of his ability, he convinces you, so that you cannot expel him now he has permeated you. In your body he came through your pores. In your mind he comes back at every turn and stoop.

You know he had a long trail of female conquests - he made no secret of it. Yet you know why you let him in. You have never met anyone like him.

To you he is lost, vulnerable, injured by trauma, fighting with distortions of his mind. Irresistible to you. A bad boy with a flaw inflicted on him so young that he had no chance. So deep he had no escape.

He looks into your eyes as if he knows what hurt is. 'Are you lonely?'

'Yes,' you reply, unable to stop the emotion rising.

'Are you isolated?'

'Very.'

'Are you a freak?'

'No.'

He holds you at arm's length, tenderly but cautiously, as if you are some unstable explosive. 'Two out of three in common, so that isn't bad.'

'Why do you think you're a freak?'

'I don't think it. I can't deny it. I can't show it isn't so. Look at me, you have access to my records, you can find out what's happened to me, what I've done, you must know I'm a freak.'

'I haven't looked up your records.'

'Maybe you should have, otherwise you might be seduced by a freak.'

'Too late for that I fear – my mind, my spirit are already seduced,' you say.

'And your body, is that weak too?'

'I would not say it is weak,' you say.

You feel the pause; you feel a growing confidence in him.

'I would not call it a weakness,' you say again.

'Sorry, who is seducing whom?' he asks with a grin.

'It started off with you seducing me but maybe you started playing hard to get – all this freak business, so I thought I should do some of the work.'

'You women – you are so good at picking up the pieces. But at least you are honest with me. At least, I think you are.'

'What do you mean?' you say, a question you use a lot with John Smith.

'That you are just as keen on the body stuff as you are on the mind and spirit.'

You laugh, 'So you can detect my arousal?'

'Of course – I can see it, hear it and smell it. I'd like to touch it too.'

For a time, you experience commotion in a similar way that John Smith must – you have an intensity of feelings from that night that fade as sensations but remain as fundamental memories. Obviously, your relationship with John Smith changes but so too does your perception of the world. A sense of urgency to make the most of what you've found. A freedom that your background has restrained from you.

That night and many others when you are both free and available result in this new life inside you. A new life that is spawned from John Smith, and many combined moments of madness.

The day you find out that John is planning the destruction of Colossus you want to confront him, to see if you can save him. You never get the chance. He knows, and you are discarded.

You hurt. As though your breast is torn off and your heart pumping, your mind and body starved of blood and life; your body is pain, your mind torment.

In the darkness of your mind you wonder who told John Smith you knew his plans; was it Colin? Was it Colossus himself? It couldn't be David. The more you think about it, the more likely it seems that they were either stolen from Colossus or Colossus decided to tell him. But you care less about that than living. Living is a struggle. You stop thinking about why John Smith has stopped coming to see you.

You start thinking of what has changed for you since you met John Smith. Everything. You cannot look at the world and think it is the same place. It has changed because of what you now know and it is changing to become a world suitable for John Smith. Things being changed in the name of freedom for him are going to result in a loss of freedom for you, and most of the rest of humankind. Inside you, sometimes, when you are very quiet and still in the bath you are just able to detect the life there. These changes - will they bring more freedom or less freedom for that life?

No. You come to a decision. You can't face the thought.

This is the time; you are starting to grieve for yourself so it must be time to go.

You walk with the robot talking to Colossus for the last time.

9.5§Alice at the end

The Change Control Committee have been working overtime; all direct circuits have been migrated from me to Colossus-19. The committee has agreed my shutdown programme. I have also been granted leave to use a robot, a 9000 series, to visit Alice Noble in her place of work – the University. The robot is making its way along the corridors of the University; it is under my direct control but of course I share all the information with Colossus-19.

I can see through the eyes of the 9000. This 9000 also has the other sensors enabling me to pick up people's subconscious, helping me detect lies and human feelings, the very tools I had used to defeat the enemy within, the Allegiance. Colossus-18 has been scrapped and Colossus-19 is up and running, working well, passing all tests with alacrity.

I can see through the eyes of the robot as we approach the door of Alice Noble's office. The robot knocks firmly and Alice calls us in; she is expecting us. She speaks before I can speak, while the robot sits on a rather flimsy chair.

'So are you under the direct control of Colossus-17?'

'Yes,' I replied, 'I am Colossus-17 speaking to you as if we had met in one of the Institute offices.'

I could see the reflection of the robot in a glass door, it was squat, only just over five feet and made to be as non-threating as possible with somewhat childish curves and cuddly shapes, which together with smiles gave the impression of helpfulness. In fact, the robot is a very powerful machine but programmed and controlled to never pose a threat to humans.

'So, Colo, how are you feeling about your project?' she asked, using her affectionate name for me.

'It is almost complete; as soon as I have finished talking to you my final shutdown will commence.'

'So why make this your last task?' she was curious, but I also sensed she was wary.

'Well I suppose the prosaic answer is that it has been a very busy time for me and Colossus-19 to complete the handover, but also since you resigned I wanted to ensure that we had got to the bottom of the Allegiance and to make sure we had developed a strategy to defend against this sort of attack. Closure.' I paused and then asked, 'how is your work? And are you tempted to go and see John Smith again?' She winced at the mention of John Smith's name but answered the questions in order. I sensed from her brain activity she knew the importance of the second question and that this question was why I had come to see her.

'My work is not very fulfilling. I will never ever go and see John Smith – after you uncovered what he was doing I began to see he was just manipulating me for his own ends - for his view on freedom and humankind. I was desperately in love with him, I have never met anyone else like him,' she struggled to go on. 'I don't agree with the idea of Aipotu – I don't think it will work. I think the evil you see in John Smith will be multiplied many times in the virtual reality. I know it sounds like histrionics, but it is pure evil. He is very cunning and he's fooled you too.'

I saw some very unusual brain patterns but I was sure she was telling the truth; what she believed to be the truth, at least.

I tried to probe a bit. 'He's a very clever sociopath. When I first warned you of the danger, before I had proof, I was worried he may detect you were beginning to suspect. He seems to have an uncanny way of knowing what people are thinking.'

She looked into the far distance and replied, 'Not unlike you then, really. I remember that day, it was like a physical blow when you warned me. I've had so much time to think it over. I always wonder why you didn't go directly to the Minister.' I wondered what she thought about the baby – why she had not terminated it. But she changed the subject, 'would you like to take a walk down to the lakeside? I don't have any lectures this afternoon.'

I agreed. The robot lifted himself effortlessly from the chair and we made our way down to the lake. There was a park seat and we made ourselves comfortable. She continued speaking about the time when she was still Chief Analyst, 'I did everything I could to ensure that the Collossus-18 project would be a success but to see that so many in the Institute were involved in trying to destroy it – in particular Colin together with John Smith, who I was so close to, it was undermining everything I believed in. I can never really understand the way Smith's mind works but I don't think he would have expected me to suspect him. Or maybe it would've made no difference to him what I thought by then.'

I sensed Alice's bodily and brain functions spiking. Suddenly, they were showing alarming signs. Through the

9000, I grasped Alice's wrist and asked her, 'Is everything okay – are you ill?'

'I am not physically ill, only sick of mind,' she replied. From that moment, the robot froze as I swamped it with instructions. As soon as I could I asked,

'What have you done? Are you about to end your life?'

She replied, 'You are at the end of yours as you've succeeded in your task; don't deny me the end of mine as I've failed in mine.'

'I cannot through inaction allow you to come to harm – there is a helicopter on its way already. In any case yours is a living life; mine is just electrical circuits.'

'Mine is too – just biological. But you are too late. I am glad you are here with me, Colo, at the end,' she said.

'You have freedom of thought. What you do may be determined but you can think what you want. I am totally determined in both thoughts and actions,' I said.

She smiled weakly, 'You're right. That makes it easier.'

The robot could not react fast enough for me. It picked her up in its arms and walked back up the hill to the waiting helicopter but I knew that life passed out of her then.

She will not see John Smith again.

In a few milliseconds - as soon as this account is complete, my shutdown will commence.

9.6§Colossus-19

In the helicopter, the infant Nobel is removed in time from Alice Nobel's lifeless body. The infant is in intensive care on a life support system - the chances of his survival are good. A robot is on its way to Zoie and Snake to see if they will adopt the infant.

I, Colossus-19, have taken over from Colossus-17.

In the confluence of life, man-made and human, time just goes on, for now.

Printed in Great Britain
by Amazon